THE LAST BIG FAKE

Kate Kerns

www.BOROUGHSPUBLISHINGGROUP.com

THE LAST BIG FAKE
Copyright © 2021 Kate Kerns

ISBN: 978-1-953810-45-8

For Zoe, who started a company with me during a pandemic and always leaves supportive comments in the margins.

ACKNOWLEDGMENTS

A huge thank you to Zoe Maffitt, whose brilliant and kind editing improves everything I write, and who got *The Last Big Fake* ready to pitch to publishers. Thank you to Eliza Bertrand, who advised on art history, France, and why she loves Monet's gardens so much. All mistakes are very much my own.

Thank you to the team at Boroughs Publishing Group for everything.

Lastly, thank you to all my friends and family who cheered me on. It's easy to believe in love when you're surrounded by it.

THE LAST BIG FAKE

Chapter One

Darcy

Sixty-three seconds after my life fell apart I crashed into a tall, handsome man. I'd been heading into the office building where I usually met the contact to whom I sold my art forgeries. When I spotted a bunch of people in the lobby wearing the telltale FBI blue jackets with gold lettering, I pivoted on my heel like the good little art criminal I was. Six years in New York's underground art world had made me fast, observant, and untrusting.

I was peeking over my shoulder to see if anyone was following me when I ran smack into a tall, thin, elegant, polished man with discrete glasses framing his brilliantly blue eyes. I scrambled to grab up my dropped things, fully expecting him to keep walking. People dressed this rich didn't stop to talk to people like me.

He bent to help and apologized in a clipped British accent.

When he passed me my butcher-paper-wrapped forgery, our fingers touched, and I got the kind of disorienting thrill you get when you're scared of heights and stand too close to the edge of a cliff.

He froze, looked at me, then blinked, like he hadn't noticed me before, but he was noticing me now. Then he did the worst thing of all.

He smiled.

If he'd asked me to drop everything and run away with him right then and there, I would've said yes. It was that kind of day, and I was that kind of lost, and he was that kind of hot.

I'd needed someone to see me, to be kind to me, and show me the world could be good again.

He saw the art book I'd dropped, and asked in an offhanded way if I happened to be looking for a job. I said yes because I needed one of those too.

That's how Seth Moreau rescued me from a life of genteel crime and forgery. Not that he knows it. To him, I'm Darcy Smith, the administrative assistant who's been giving him good advice, bad coffee, and mild heart attacks for the last two years. Darcy Sherwood, failed-art-student turned brilliant-art-forger doesn't exist anymore.

I open the Moreau Gallery's back door with my hip since my arms are loaded with priceless, thoroughly ugly paintings. After putting the paintings in the storeroom, I brush the dust off my white silk shirt and head into the back offices. Seth's dark, tailored coat hangs on the coat hook, and his quiet, no-nonsense voice drifts out into the hall. My desk sits right outside his office. The rest of the staff are in shared space down the hall, closer to the gallery.

I hang my coat and hat next to his. Crushed purple velvet next to sober black wool. I start the coffee then check the messages on my office phone while scrolling through my emails on my cell to make sure nothing's on fire.

At the request of his great-aunt Amelie, a stern French woman I've spoken to only over the phone, and who scares the living daylights out of me, I leave Seth one free night a week for dating, even though he doesn't seem to use it. One time he had me send flowers to a woman, but it was to apologize for canceling on her.

I'm one to talk. Hiding a past as an art forger tends to get in the way of forming meaningful relationships, romantic or otherwise. It's a bad sign when late-night office takeout with your boss is the highlight of your social calendar.

I click on a link about an art auction, then blink. No way. A piece Seth's been trying to get forever is going up for sale.

"Hey, Seth," I call. I slosh some coffee into his favorite mug and hurry into his office. "Seth, the Dizzy Lizzy's going up for auction—"

He glances up from his screen. "Not now, Darcy."

"What do you mean not now? It's the Dizzy Lizzy. You love that painting. I'm pretty sure your cold little cash box heart has wet dreams about that painting."

"Darcy," he says, sounding strained. "Language. Please."

"Seth? Who is that?" an old lady's voice asks from Seth's computer speakers. Seth looks at the ceiling.

"No one, Aunt Amelie. Only my assistant." He looks over the monitor at me and mouths "FaceTime," somewhat unnecessarily.

"Drat. I was hoping it was a woman," Aunt Amelie says.

I lean over to hand him his coffee. Our fingers brush, and Seth jumps, spilling coffee down his crisp blue shirt. He leaps out of his chair and his face goes tense and white, but he doesn't yelp or swear like a normal person. It would be beneath him. It doesn't matter. I'm swearing enough for the both of us. It has to be scalding him.

I grab a Kleenex and start dabbing at his shirt. "Really, Darcy. Stop. You don't need to," Seth says, his voice strained again. His voice is often strained around me.

"Take it off," I say. "I've got your dry-cleaning in the closet. I bet I could get the stain out with a Tide stick."

"That's not necessary."

"At the price you pay for shirts, it absolutely is. Take off the shirt."

"I will not."

"You're wearing an undershirt."

For some reason, he blushes, then crosses his arms over his chest.

Like that will stop me from noticing he's blushing. I put my hands on my hips. The man is ridiculous. We glare at each other. He's so *aggravating*.

"Well. This explains a lot," Aunt Amelie says.

Seth breaks eye contact with me. "What are you talking about?"

"Oh, my dear boy," Amelie says airily. "Everything. The stuff of heaven, and the stuff of hell. The golden thread which makes life worth living."

Seth rolls his eyes and settles back in his chair. I gather she talks like this a lot.

I should leave, but I can't resist sneaking a peek at the infamous Amelie. Her gray hair is elegantly swept up, and she's wearing a simple gray sweater with trim beige slacks. She's got a brilliant blue scarf wrapped around her head, and she's lounging regally on an antique silk couch.

I grin. I think I like Aunt Amelie. To my surprise, she pins me with a sharp look. Then she smiles right back. "Yes," she says softly to herself. "This will do nicely."

"Amelie, if you're going to mutter cryptically…" Seth warns. She swivels her focus to him. "You said you wanted to talk about something important."

"Yes. Yes I did. It's about my will."

He straightens, alarmed. "Are you sick? I can be on a plane in a minute." Seth means it. I'm already booking flights in my head.

Amelie laughs. Her laugh is a peal of bells, if bells went to Parisian finishing schools. "I'm fine, darling. I've made a decision about your inheritance."

Seth relaxes. "Amelie, you know I don't care about that. Whatever you want to do."

"If you don't get married within the year, everything goes to your brother."

"What?" Seth asks, clearly stunned. "Wait, you mean the *money*. You're designating the chateau as a public museum."

"No, I'm giving the chateau to your brother."

"But you're giving the art collection—"

"To your brother, yes." Amelie nods encouragingly.

"But why would you…" Seth trails off. "It's *Victor*."

"Yes, well the thing is, I don't want my house to become a museum. I want it to stay in the family. Which is why I'm leaving the house and the collection to whichever one of you gets married within the year."

"But—" Seth starts, but he stops when Amelie holds up a hand.

"I'd recommend you look around at your life. Start making use of the date night your beautiful assistant leaves open on the calendar."

She thinks I'm beautiful? I'm flattered. It's like the fairy godmother shows up in *Cinderella*. She's terrifying and French, and instead of giving a makeover she tells Cinderella she was good enough as she is.

"*Au revoir*, darling," Amelie says and ends the call.

Seth's expression screams hurt and confused. I don't know why he hates his brother, but I'm pretty sure Amelie knew her ultimatum would feel like a stab in the back.

Seth, who calls her every week. Seth, who was willing to drop everything and get on a plane when he thought she was sick, no matter how many missed deals and money it would cost him. Seth, who didn't blink when he thought she was writing him out of her will to give it all to charity.

His brilliant blue eyes flash. "What the hell just happened?"

Chapter Two

Seth

I don't know why it's worse Darcy witnessed it all, but somehow it is. I know she thinks I'm a stuffed shirt. Everything about Darcy is stamped "free spirit," from her wild brown curls to the vintage silk clinging to her curves, to the high-heeled red suede boots, which disappear under her shin-length skirt, but go up to her thighs. It's like someone designed her wardrobe as a personal attack on my sanity.

Nope. Don't think about Darcy. Thinking about Darcy is like admiring the retro neon sign on the strip club behind the gallery. Inevitable, but also not something you want to be caught doing or people will get the wrong impression.

If I don't get married within the year, a chateau in Burgundy, which has been in my family for two hundred years, is going to my brother, who will either sell it to the highest bidder or do something awful like renting it out to shoot pornos.

I don't even want to think about what he'll do to the art filling it.

Should I sign up for online dating? I'm not opposed to getting married. I've always assumed one of these days I'd meet the perfect woman, fall in love, etcetera. Someone elegant, honest, and smart. The type of woman I'm thinking of needs at least a year to *plan* a wedding, let alone decide she wants me. And a wedding means…forever.

By the time I find someone I like, Amelie will have signed everything over to Victor.

I close my eyes and rub my forehead.

"Drink your coffee," Darcy says. "You'll feel better."

"Not if you made it."

I hear the click of her heels walking toward the door, and I'm disappointed and relieved at the same time. None of my previous assistants questioned me as much as Darcy does. When she first started working here, she'd purse her lips and raise her brows whenever she disagreed with my decisions. I could've ignored her, but instead I gave in and asked what she thought about this client, that vendor, those paintings. Until she stopped waiting for me to ask.

Darcy's opinions can be a pain, but they've also saved me from making some bad mistakes. Like a business deal with a famous artist who was later outed as a bigot. She sees things I don't. She refuses to let me look away.

Darcy's also the one who comes up with unconventional solutions when I am completely, utterly stumped.

Her steps hesitate at the door. "There's no way you can talk sense into her?"

Maybe Darcy's not walking out after all. I look up, trying not to feel hopeful. "No. Once she makes up her mind, she's set."

"You can't talk her down to an engagement?"

I shake my head.

Darcy bites her lip. She does it when she's thinking. It's the kind of thing that would be horribly distracting if a man were into her. I bet she wins every argument she's ever had with her boyfriend.

Don't stare at the neon lights, I remind myself. Even if she didn't work for me, Darcy Smith is the opposite of everything I'm looking for in a woman.

Well, not the *complete* opposite. She's smart, beautiful, loyal, competent, and secretly—she'd yell at me for saying this—incredibly kind. But Darcy is not a restful woman. She's volcanic enough at work. I can't imagine what she'd be like off the clock.

"Okay," Darcy says slowly, drawing out the word. "She wants you to get married because she wants you to have kids. Maybe you could skip the marriage thing and knock someone up?"

"Are you offering?" I ask dryly.

"What? No. Why would you say that?"

"I'm pointing out how ridiculous it is. Even if I did want to bring a child into this world, to keep a house, what am I supposed to do? Walk up to a woman in a club and say hello, nice to meet you, would you like to have my children?"

Darcy looks me up and down and smirks in a way that raises the hairs on the back of my neck. "That might be more effective than you think."

"Miss Smith," I scold. Darcy smooths her face into a contrite expression, but there's a wicked glint in her eye. I'm not sure when it started, but at some point, "Miss Smith" became shorthand for "you've crossed a line, please be professional." I believe "Mr. Moreau" means the same thing, but she uses it so rarely, I'm not sure.

I rise and start pacing. Every idea I come up with is stupider than the last. I know this because sometimes I say them out loud, and Darcy shoots them down with increasing speed.

"Shit. Bugger. *Fuck.*" I give my desk a vicious kick. Darcy looks at me as if I'd shot a dog. This is what happens when you try to be perfect. When you crack, even a little, people judge you all the harsher for it.

Meanwhile, Victor spends his life acting like a selfish fucker and Aunt Amelie gives him the family inheritance to crush in his greedy thumbs.

"I'm sorry," I grit out. "This isn't work-related. I shouldn't've involved you. Feel free to return to your desk. I've got the Lageson meeting in an hour—"

"You could lie," Darcy blurts.

I double blink. "What?"

"Say you've found someone. Introduce her over FaceTime. Then say you're engaged. Then say you're married. Wait until Amelie signs it all over to you, wait a few months. Then tell her you got divorced."

"You want me to lie. To someone I love. For *a year*."

Darcy shrugs and makes a I-know-I'm-a-bad-person-but-I-don't-actually-feel-guilty face other people make when they forget to bring their reusable grocery bags to the store.

I never forget to bring my reusable bags.

"I can't do that to her."

"Victor's going to," Darcy says ruthlessly, and I flinch.

She's right. I know she's right. But... "I don't want to manipulate someone I love."

"Why not?" Darcy says. "She's manipulating you."

She turns and goes back to her desk, leaving me standing in the wreckage of the weirdest Tuesday morning of my life.

***

That night, I toss and turn as I'm trying to fall asleep. I can't get Darcy's voice out of my head. Without meaning to, I start planning what I'd need to pull off the lie.

I'd need a woman who was comfortable lying, who wouldn't get weird about it and think I was genuinely interested. Someone pretty enough, and smart enough Amelie would believe I'm in love with her. Ideally, someone Amelie already knows I know, so it's kind of believable when I get engaged.

My eyes fly open.

Darcy.

***

It takes a week of Amelie asking if I've found someone yet, and Victor texting to tell me how much the chateau next to Amelie's sold for before I crack and stride into the office with an engagement ring in my pocket.

For once, Darcy's at work before me. Probably because it took longer than I thought to pick out the right fake engagement ring.

She's a hard woman to shop for.

I throw down a green velvet ring box on her desk.

Darcy's hands freeze on the keyboard. She looks at the box, then slowly up at me. "Well, good morning to you too."

"I'll do it. But only if it's you," I say.

Her dark brows furrow. "Do what?"

"Lie. About the engagement. To Amelie. To beat Victor. I'll do it. But only if you're the fake fiancée."

She reaches for the box. "Why me?"

"I get the feeling you can lie," I say, and she winces.

"I don't mean it's a bad thing," I hasten to add. "In this case."

Darcy makes a face. Then she flips open the box, and her expression softens. "Oh, Seth. It's beautiful."

She lifts the ring from the box and holds it up to catch the light. It has an antique silver band, and whatever the original jewels were have been replaced by an asymmetrical rainbow of emerald and sapphire and amethyst, all of it setting off a center ruby making me think of Darcy's scarlet boots.

Well, her boots and her mouth.

"If you lie to Amelie, you can keep the ring," I say.

"Why, Mr. Moreau," Darcy says. "How perfectly manipulative of you."

There's a note of approval in her voice, but the shame is hot on the back of my neck, and I feel low and foolish. "Never mind, forget I asked." I grab the ring, but Darcy snatches it back and jams it on her left ring finger.

"Don't you dare. I love this ring. I've bonded with this ring. This ring and I are ready for our close-up." Darcy holds her left hand up next to her face and mimes waving to a camera, and I crack a smile.

If anyone could pull this off, it's Darcy. It also makes me feel better she approves of the ring and my decision. Her morality may be a little chaotic—I once caught her sticking a forged parking ticket on the windshield of one particularly rude customer's Ferrari—but it's definitely there.

Maybe I'm not the worst person in the world to be considering this. To be *doing* this.

"So," Darcy says. "How long have we been in love, and when do you want to tell Amelie?"

"Today. I want to get this over with," I say.

Darcy nods and bites her lip, running through our options.

Ten minutes later, we've decided we've been dating for a year. We haven't told anyone because of our professional relationship, but since it matters so much to Amelie, we've decided to make it public. Darcy keeps trying to go off into wild, romantic flights of fancy, but I argue we should keep it as simple and truthful as possible.

"How did you ask me to marry you?" Darcy asks.

"I went down on one knee and said, 'Will you marry me?'"

Darcy looks dissatisfied. "Okay. But where were you? Was it at a baseball game in front of hundreds of people, or on a mountain overlooking the sunset? Or—"

"It was in the office," I say, and she throws her hands up in the air, exasperated.

"That is the lamest proposal story I ever heard."

I don't say anything.

"Fine," Darcy relents. "But you were naked."

"*What?*"

"You were overcome with desire one night after a gallery opening. We boinked like bunnies, you saw stars, and proposed."

"I am not telling my great-aunt *that*." I cross my arms.

"No of course not. We'll tell her your boring version, but you'll be thinking of my version when you tell it, and she'll see in your eyes there's more to the story, and that's the kind of detail that makes the difference between a good liar and a bad one." Darcy checks something on her computer, while I stare at her, horrified and impressed.

I'm beginning to have some suspicions about how she can always get me on anyone's calendar, no matter how busy and influential they are.

"What's the time difference between here and France again?" Darcy asks, like we haven't been discussing anything more interesting than the weather. "Because you're booked solid from ten a.m. to eight p.m."

***

In the end, we decide it's easiest to take some fake engagement pictures and simply send them to Amelie. Darcy can't find a way to make the time zones work with my calendar, and I don't think my lying skills are up to it. Even with Darcy's embarrassingly descriptive "boinking like bunnies" lurking in the back of my brain.

Around four-thirty p.m., Darcy comes into my office and locks the door behind her. I look up sharply.

"What are you doing?"

"You've got eighteen minutes until your next call, and the lighting's good right now. Let's get these engagement pictures over with."

"Um... Okay." It will be over faster if I let Darcy run this. "Should I stand or...?"

Darcy surveys the room, surveys me, bites her lip—god, that fucking lip—then shakes her head.

"No, you sit at your desk."

Slowly, I lower myself into my chair. "Where are you going to sit?"

"On your lap," she says, stepping toward me. I wheel the chair back automatically until I bash into the wall. "What? No. That's unprofessional."

Darcy puts her hands on her hips. "Seth. Marriage is by definition unprofessional."

I stare back, sullen.

Darcy taps her foot. Today she's in hot pink patent leather sky-high heels with gold tips across the pointed toe. I've never *dated* anyone with hot pink shoes, let alone gotten engaged to them.

"Seth," she says in her "I'm the real boss" tone she uses when she thinks I'm being an idiot. She watched an online seminar a few months ago, and now she calls it "managing up." "Do you want your aunt to believe us?"

"Yes."

"Then imagine you were in love with me, and I said yes. Now we're taking photos we'll use to tell everyone we care about we're going to be happy for the rest of our damn lives. Obviously, we can't keep our hands off each other."

I don't say anything.

She's in a simple straight cream skirt today, but it's short, shorter than she usually wears, and Darcy may be a thorn in my otherwise neatly pruned life, but her legs are... I swallow. I know she's trying to be helpful, but I don't think this whole her in my lap thing is such a great idea.

Darcy tilts her head, an effect exaggerated by the way all her hair swings with her. "Actually, I could be behind you, sort of draped around your back."

An image of Darcy pressing her breasts into my back, laughing into my ear, her hair tangling around me, pops into my head. I'm not into her. I'm not, but it's been a while since I had sex, and some part of me wants to say "Yes, please." I clear my throat and push up my glasses. "You've made your point. My lap is a reasonable location given the relationship dynamics we're trying to portray."

"Given the relationship dynamics we're trying to portray," Darcy mimics, but she directs me to a spot where we'll get the best light, then settles into my lap and pulls out her phone.

I'm inhaling the scent of her hair, surprised to find she smells fresh, lemony—I would have expected something showier—when she snaps the first picture.

Darcy frowns at the picture, and I freeze, thinking I've been caught, when she turns and looks at me critically. She lifts a hand like she's going to fix my hair, then hesitates. "May I?"

"Go ahead," I say.

She runs a hand through my hair, and the light pressure of her fingertips against my scalp feels…intimate. I can't remember the last time I've been touched like this. Even when I was seeing someone, I was always the one doing the seducing. The caretaking. The chasing. If my ex touched me outside of the bedroom, it would have only been to slick a hair back into place.

That's not what Darcy's doing. She's…messing me up. In more ways than one.

She finishes with my hair, then loosens my tie. "Roll up your sleeves," she orders.

"Trying to make it look like you had your way with me?" I ask dryly, but I do what she says.

"No. I'm trying to make it look like you're actually happy." She lifts her phone and starts snapping pictures of us. She scrolls through the photos. "None of these are right. You look stiff. Like you don't even like me. Why do you look so weird?"

Because you smell amazing and you're squirming around an inch from my dick and I'm trying not to get a hard-on.

"How about I take the picture?" I take the phone from her. "So you can show off your ring."

"Not every woman shows off her ring in the engagement photo."

"True. But you would."

Darcy thinks about it. "Okay. Yeah, I would."

When I lift the camera, I use it as an excuse to shift Darcy farther to the side. When she tries to wiggle, I hold my hand firm to get her to stop moving—please god, let her stop moving—and to my surprise, she does.

Instead, she melts into me, leaning her head against my shoulder, while she grins mischievously and flashes her ring to the camera. I can't help but smile because it's so fundamentally Darcy. If a man were in love with Darcy, this is exactly the way he'd hold her.

I snap a photo and show it to Darcy, who's strangely quiet.

"That's it," she says at last. "That's the one."

She hops off my lap so suddenly I feel cold. "Send it to Amelie. Your phone meeting is in five minutes."

She fumbles with the doorknob, before she remembers she locked it, and scurries out the door.

Okay. That was weird.

I shake it off and send the photo to Amelie. Then I go back to work, calling a potential buyer I need to woo. I'm fifteen minutes into the call and developing a crick in my neck from holding the desk phone between my shoulder and my ear while typing before I get a text back from Amelie.

Oh, wonderful! I knew you two were perfect together.

I roll my eyes. Talk about seeing something that isn't there.

Come to the chateau for the month, so I can get to know her better.

This month? I text back. *Unfortunately, I can't clear my schedule.*

You could do it when you thought I was dying, she shoots back.

Darcy can't take the time off, I type.

She works for you. I'm about to launch into an explanation of how complicated the contemporary art ecosystem is when Aunt Amelie texts again. *If I didn't know you better, I'd think you didn't want to bring her because you weren't really engaged, and you're scared if you both stay with me for a month, I'll find out.*

Well, shit.

Maybe Darcy could have found a way out of this, but instinctively I type *Of course not. We could absolutely spend a month with you.*

The response is instant. *Magnifique! Arrive next Tuesday. I'm making lamb.*

I feel a surge of triumph Amelie believed me, followed by the emotional plummet of realizing what an absolute idiot I've been.

I pinch the bridge of my nose and slump in my chair while the buyer continues to yammer on about the aesthetics of disruption. I hope Darcy wants a free vacation in Burgundy.

If she doesn't, I am well and truly fucked.

Chapter Three

Darcy Sherwood

I breathe a sigh of relief as I make it through JFK security, then check my watch. I've got an hour and a half until my plane takes off.

Nervous, I drum my fingers on the handle of my suitcase. I've been to a handful of contemporary art hubs working for Seth. Miami, LA, Hong Kong. In college, I'd hop a bus with my friends to whatever random city had cheap tickets that weekend. We'd get drunk and wander the streets taking photos. We'd eat dessert for breakfast and breakfast at midnight, calling it research for the big, artistic lives we planned to live.

I haven't talked to those friends in forever. Partly it's envy of their careers, and of their relationships. Mostly it's my criminal past and fake name. I push past the familiar pang of loneliness. I don't get to have the secure happy ever after surrounded by friends and family who know and love the real me. I get to have the adventure. And today, it's a damn good adventure.

I check my boarding pass for my gate. This is going to be my first trip to Europe. Not only Europe. France. It's been years since I held a brush. When Seth proposed an all-expenses-paid vacation, I could feel Darcy Sherwood rising to the surface. A chance to see the land of Renoir, Cézanne, Morisot.

To see Monet.

Still, I hesitated. It would be a bad enough idea if it was any old boss. But it's *Seth*. The man who's perceptive enough to buy me the most perfect ring in the history of the universe, and obtuse enough not to realize he should actually, you know, *smile* in his fake engagement photos.

Although when he finally figured it out... God, the man can smile.

I shake my head. The fact Seth Moreau needs a fake fiancé proves modern love makes no fucking sense. I'm not saying I'd ever fall in love with him. The man probably folds his socks neatly before sex. But in another life, I would so hit on him in a bar. If you'd do that, you don't pretend to be their fiancée for a month in France. That's pretty much Protecting Your Heart & Dignity 101.

I was about to turn him down—Darcy Smith wanted to keep her great job more than Darcy Sherwood wanted to see Europe—when Seth did the unthinkable. He cleared his throat and looked at the ground and said, "Please."

His entreaty pretty much did it. Because it's not some hypothetical guy in a bar. It's Seth. Aggravating, principled, controlled Seth, backed into a corner with his family because he followed my advice.

I mean, I still played hard to get long enough to get a day trip to see Monet's gardens in Giverny. I'm not a saint.

Officially, this is a work trip so Seth can check in with a Paris gallery we have a partnership with. I was able to reassign most of his meetings to other staff members, and the rest of his work will be conducted remotely from his aunt's villa. I worked sixty hours last week to line it all up.

Now I have a suitcase full of sundresses, a carry-on full of romance novels, and a month in France stretching out before me. I sigh happily and saunter to my gate, which, it turns out, is near a wine bar. I find a spot at the bar and order a glass of prosecco. I might as well start the vacation off right.

I'm sipping my bubbly and scrolling through a list of things to see in Burgundy when a deep voice speaks from behind me.

"Beautiful women should never drink alone."

A chill crawls up my spine. No. Not here. I haven't seen V since I became Darcy Smith.

I take a sip of my wine as if his appearance hasn't sent a sick chill down my spine.

"You're right, we shouldn't." I turn to face him. "When we do, people like you talk to us."

The man laughs. "So it *is* you. I haven't seen you in forever, Robin."

I flinch. It's V all right. His blond haircut is way trendy, and his eyes have gotten harder, but he's still got the same Hollywood vampire meets fallen British gentry vibe. Designer jeans, black velvet jacket.

Then there's my nickname. No one went by their real names in our little forgery ring. I didn't know at first. I thought it was a real job interview, and V genuinely wanted to commission some impressionist-inspired art for himself.

He thought my flub was adorable, so he took it upon himself to pick my cover name: Robin Hood. A reference to my real last name, and the fact we were robbing the rich.

Though we weren't giving to the poor. Not unless you counted the various poor artists who forged for V.

I hated, *hated*, he knew my real name. It wasn't enough he took painting from me. He literally stole my name.

"What do you want?" I demand.

"Can't a fellow say hi to an old colleague?"

"You're not a colleague. You're a mistake." I drop some cash on the bar to cover my drink, grab my bags, and head to my gate. I smell the stale scent of cigarettes underneath his expensive cologne as I squeeze past him.

"Ah, come now, Robin. Don't be like that." He chases after me and grabs my arm.

I whirl. "Let go of me," I say, voice raised. "I don't know you. Stop touching me."

Other travelers are looking at us now. V narrows his eyes. "That was idiotic. You don't want attention any more than I do."

I jerk my arm. "Then *let go*."

A short, solid, kind-faced man in an airport security uniform jogs up, faintly out of breath. "Is there a problem, ma'am?"

"This drunk man keeps saying he knows me. I'm sure he's confused and doesn't mean any harm." I look down at V's hand on my arm meaningfully.

V releases my arm. "Sorry, officer. My mistake."

"Oh, I'm not really an officer—"

V's already walking away.

The airport security man gives me a kind look. "Are you sure you're all right?"

No, I think. *That was too much of a coincidence.*

***

There's a bunch of high-schoolers waiting at the gate for our flight, plus tourists and businesspeople. Normally I don't like noisy, tightly packed crowds, but it's a relief to weave through everyone, putting bodies between V and me.

I'm fine until I spot Seth typing on a laptop over by the windows, headphones in, his luggage tucked neatly beside him. The noise, sound, and scent of the airport rush in on me and my hands start shaking. He glances up, reflexively. As soon as he sees me, his eyes sharpen, and he yanks his headphones out.

"What's wrong?" He moves toward me.

I open my mouth, then close it. Some primal part of my brain wants to tell him what happened, so I can feel safe. But if I tell Seth the truth, he won't be on my side.

"Darcy." He runs his hands up and down my arms, like he's trying to rub life back into me. Strange. He never touches me. I touch him, but he never touches me. "Darcy, please talk to me. Tell me what's wrong."

I shake my head and step away from him. "It's not a big deal. A man got aggressive." Thunderclouds form over Seth's face. "Not aggressive-aggressive. He thought I was someone else and it made me think about things I haven't thought about for a while. I'm fine."

He studies me like a doctor studying a patient, and I try to radiate wellness. He gives me a look like he knows what I'm doing. Instead of calling me on my crap, he guides me back to where he's sitting and starts asking incredibly simple questions about work he should really know himself.

I sit and answer on autopilot. It helps to talk about something normal. Something safe. Something I'm good at. He passes me a water bottle and I take a swig automatically. When I lower the bottle, I realize my hands have stopped shaking.

Seth reaches out his hand like he wants to touch me again, but he pulls back at the last second. "Let me know if you want to talk."

I nod and drink more water. He goes back to his laptop, but he doesn't put his headphones in, and he keeps sneaking glances at me.

I people-watch while he types. By the time a voice announces first class can board, I'm thinking maybe seeing V *is* a coincidence.

We both live in New York City, and we both travel in art circles. It was only a matter of time. Running into V in a public place gives nothing away about my current life. Doing it right before I leave the country for a month is probably the best way this could've worked out.

"I still think you should have let us travel first class," I nag Seth. "What's the point of being rich if you're not going to fly first class on a transatlantic flight?"

"How do you think I got rich?" Seth doesn't look up from his computer, but there's a flicker of a smile in the corner of his mouth.

I stand and start to gather our bags when I see my worst nightmare. V, sauntering toward the gate. A tall blond with leopard print pants and skyscraper heels is on his arm, giggling as she takes in everyone around her.

I freeze, and Seth notices. "What's going—"

"He's here."

Seth tenses. He stands, and I'm reminded of how tall he is. He looks formidable. "Where?" he demands, and for the first time in my life, I can picture him in a bar fight.

"It's really fine."

"Darcy."

I point, and Seth goes still. Across the room, V is looking from me to Seth, equally stunned. It's like they know each other, but that makes no sense. Seth is as upright as they come, and V is the slime of the earth. They're both sculpted, white, British men in their early thirties, but that's where the similarities end.

Still, the way they're looking at each other, it's like the leopard-print woman and I aren't even here.

"Do you know him?" I ask Seth.

"That," he says grimly, "is my brother."

Chapter Four

Darcy

V is Victor Moreau. Based on the size of the rock on the giggly blonde's left hand, my guess is he's heading to Aunt Amelie's for the same reason we are.

Shit, shit, shit, fuck, shit.

I'm spending a month with the one person who could bring my new life crashing down around my ears. The good news is, Seth hates Victor so much, he'd probably believe me over him. On the other hand, Victor is his brother, and Seth is the fairest man I've ever met, so if Victor produces proof I'm really a forger...

I take a deep breath. Victor can't share that kind of proof without exposing himself. What did he say before airport security showed up? *You don't want attention any more than I do.* This is fine. Mutually assured destruction is a totally viable strategy, as demonstrated by years of geo-global policy.

I realize this is a minor point since I'm also pissed because Victor is ruining my perfect French vacation.

Well, as perfect as a vacation can be when I'm pretending to be my boss's fiancé.

As we file past Victor and the blonde to get to our seats (Victor sprung for first class), I try to figure out how I couldn't've known.

Seth has been feuding with Victor as long as I've known him, so I never saw them together. It's not like Seth keeps photos of Victor around the office.

Victor's been in the media. Now I think about it, the photos he provides are always highly stylized. A face bisected by shadow, or stylishly hidden under the brim of a hat. Seth gives reporters the same straightforward, no-frills headshot he uses on LinkedIn.

I could have found out about Victor if I'd done any digging. But why would I? He was the older brother Seth didn't want to talk about.

We find our seats. I'm squeezed into the middle seat between a pleasant woman with aggressively large knitting needles on the window side, and a fuming Seth on the aisle side. He tries to get comfortable, but no matter what he does, his long legs jab into the seat in front of him.

The tray falls down. He puts it back up. It falls again. He slams it up with so much force a piece of plastic cracks off.

"Good thing we didn't do first class," I say.

Seth groans. "For once in your life, don't. Please don't."

I feel chagrined.

He rubs a hand over his face, then heaves a heavy sigh and looks at me. "Darcy, I'm so sorry Victor bothered you, and I dragged you into this. I am so, so sorry."

"How he behaves isn't your fault."

"No. But why he behaves that way might be."

I lean forward, thinking I'm finally going to hear why Seth and Victor hate each other—aside from the obvious fact Victor is, to use Seth's phrase, a git—but Seth glares straight ahead.

Apparently this is the end of the conversation.

We take off, and I turn the problem over in my head, trying to think through angles and strategy, but I don't have enough information. I need to find out what Victor has planned before I decide how to proceed.

Until then, there's nothing I can do. Unlike Mr. Brooding to my left, I can't stare at nothing for eight hours. It feels wrong, but there's nothing else I can do. I pull out my romance novel and tuck my brain into the fictional world like you'd tuck an exhausted child into bed, diving in to the comforting escapism of a beautiful, spunky reporter who rescues a tall, respectable duke from his boring, proper life.

***

I wake up with my cheek pressed into crisp cotton. I curl deeper under my blanket.

Blanket?

I open my eyes as the lights flick on. The flight attendant is announcing we're landing. My cheek is pressed into Seth's shoulder, and his suit jacket is draped over me.

I sit up abruptly, startling Seth, who looks up from his book.

Wait. He's reading my book.

Seth Moreau is reading my romance novel, and I'm wearing his jacket. I look from the jacket to the book in confusion. "What…?"

"Apologies. You were shivering. I tried to acquire a blanket, but they were out. We will not be flying this airline again."

Actually, we will be flying this airline in a month. I booked our return tickets.

"That's not what I meant." I fold the jacket and hand it back to him. "I meant why are you reading my book?"

"You dropped it when you were sleeping. I was bored, and I like your taste in music, so… Darcy, this is *not* realistic."

"That's the point," I say, but he ignores me to flip back to a specific spot in the book. I have a sudden fear he's going to point to one of the sex scenes, which, while hella hot, are perhaps not realistic from a male perspective.

Instead, he jabs a finger at one of the paragraphs where the characters are talking about British politics. "That is *not* how zoning laws work."

"That's *not* the point of the conversation."

"But in chapter eight—"

"LA LA LA LA LA. No spoilers." I snag the book and shove it back into my carry-on.

The plane finishes taxiing, and everyone begins collecting their things.

"My husband's horrible about spoilers too," Knitting Needles lady says knowingly.

"Oh, he's not my husband. He's my—"

"Fiancé," Seth cuts in and leans over me to shake the lady's hand. "I'm taking her to meet my aunt. Lovely flying with you."

"Well, aren't you the cutest thing," she says, shaking hands around me, and beaming up at Seth. I restrain the urge to gag.

By the time we're filing off the plane, first class has already emptied. "So we're starting the lie already?" I ask under my breath.

"Should we not?" he asks back as we walk up the carpeted tube, which leads us into the airport. "Given who we ran into earlier, it seemed wise."

"It's fine," I lie, as we emerge into the airport. It feels like the more we do this, the more we're risking our professional relationship, but Seth's probably right.

When we emerge from the plane, a cheerful Southern woman's voice says, "There they are."

Seth and I look over to see the leopard-print blonde waving at us aggressively. Next to her, Victor's trying to look bored, but he's on high alert.

Seth and I look at each other.

"I don't suppose we can pretend we didn't see them?" Seth asks. "Since we're lying anyway?"

I snort as the blonde rushes over to us. She hugs me, enveloping me in a cloud of cheap perfume. It's fast and efficient, not unlike a TSA pat-down, but with more hairspray.

Before I can react, she moves on to Seth, but he's learned from my mistake and attempts to keep her at bay with a firm handshake.

"Silly. That's no great way to greet family." She upgrades to a hug.

"Family?" Seth asks.

"Where are my manners?" She releases Seth and gestures to herself. "I'm Barbie Emerson." We stare at her. "Victor's fiancée." She holds up her left hand and giggles. She looks at me, and her eyes narrow the tiniest bit. "You are?"

I'm trying to figure out if there's a way to do this without giving Victor my new last name, but Seth must mistake my silence for uncertainty, because he wraps an arm around my waist and says, "Darcy Smith. My fiancée."

Barbie claps her hands. "Well isn't this the most perfect coincidence? How did you two meet?"

"Work," I say.

Victor smirks. "Screwing the secretary, Seth? How the mighty have fallen."

Seth's hand tightens on my waist.

"Y'all are going to Aunt Amelie's too, right?"

I don't know if Barbie is trying to smooth over the tension, or if she's genuinely oblivious.

"Correct," Seth grits out.

"You should ride with us. No sense taking two cars."

Visions of Seth going to French prison for committing murder flash in my head. I'd be okay with him murdering Victor, but Barbie seems mostly innocent.

"It's all right. We've already reserved our car, and paid the rental fee, so…" I shrug and Seth shoots me a grateful look.

"Well, perfect, 'cause we haven't rented ours yet," Barbie beams.

"It does make sense," Victor drawls. He raises a brow. "Unless there's a reason you don't want to spend time with me?"

"Of course there's a reason, you bloody arsehole," Seth says, but I cut him off.

"No reason at all. You're welcome to join us."

Seth is sending me *fuck no* signals, but I ignore him to smile brightly at Victor.

"One big, happy family," Victor says sarcastically, and Barbie claps delightedly.

***

Seth drives, and I'm going to let Victor sit up front next to him, but Seth shoots me a look which tells me I will absolutely be fired if I do. Which is how I end up riding through the French countryside, staring at lovely rolling fields and ancient stones while my mortal enemy stares daggers at the back of my neck.

When Seth glances over and says, "Almost there," in a low, comforting voice, it's one of the best sentences I've heard in my life.

We turn down a side road, but as we keep driving through sweeping trees and soft lawns, it dawns on me. This is the driveway. We pull up in front of a cream stone building with a blue roof. It's regally symmetrical, and roughly the size of a small apartment building.

"Holy shit," Barbie says. "It's a castle, y'all."

Seth says, "A chateau is not—"

"Nope. She's right. It's a castle," I say, and Victor laughs.

We all pile out of the car—Barbie has a lot of luggage—as the chateau door opens, and a small woman with a red sweater draped over her shoulders walks down the stone steps.

Amelie stops a few steps from the ground so she can survey us. "Well," she says, and there's laughter in her voice. "I see you've made it."

"Aunt Amelie…" Seth says, a warning in his voice, but Amelie ignores him and throws her arms wide open.

"Come. Forget all that and give your favorite aunt a hug."

Seth's sigh of frustration can't hide his obvious affection as he bends down to hug his aunt. He's a good head and a half taller than her, and there's something sweet about the way he bends his knees so she can properly hug him, and kiss each of his cheeks. Like those videos of large dogs letting themselves be bossed around by small cats.

Victor is next, and technically his motions are the same, but it's a duty when he does it. The contrast between the two men couldn't be more obvious.

Barbie and I share a look. Maybe Barbie's a better judge of character than I thought. Then why is she engaged to Victor? I assumed he was using her, but maybe she's in on it like I am.

"Who are these lovely ladies?" Amelie asks. Barbie and I snap to attention.

"Darcy, ma'am. We met over FaceTime. I spilled coffee on your nephew." I'm babbling.

Amelie's smile widens. "So you did. It's lovely to meet you in person." She kisses each cheek. I feel like I've stepped into a 1950s high society movie, minus the servants.

Amelie turns to Barbie. "Miss Emerson, I take it?"

"Yes, ma'am," Barbie says, and does a little curtsy like she's meeting the queen. "It's a pleasure to meet Victor's family. He speaks so highly of you."

"I'm sure he does." The corner of Amelie's mouth tightens, exactly like Seth's does when he's trying not to laugh.

Amelie turns back to the house. "Well, come on. I'll show you your rooms. The grounds are lovely at this time of day if the boys want to show you around before dinner. Seth and Victor, get the luggage."

I wink at Seth as he struggles with my stuff as well as his. If we were a real couple, I'd help. But given the amount of crap I've lugged for him over the years—the urinal sculpture comes to mind—this seems like fair play.

Victor looks at Barbie's mound of pink luggage in horror. Barbie and I follow Amelie up the steps.

"I have only three bedrooms available at the moment. We're doing some renovations on the fourth-floor rooms. I presume you'd prefer to share with your fiancés."

I look back at Seth, panicking. He'd assured me his great-aunt was way too proper to put us in the same room.

He looks up from struggling with the suitcases, alarmed. "Actually, Amelie—"

"I'm a born-again virgin," Barbie blurts. "I'll take the third room, if y'all don't mind. Saving myself for marriage." She giggles.

"You're *what*?" Victor drops the pink suitcase on his toe and swears.

"I'm not judging you," Barbie assures me. "It's really important as women we support each other's choices. I absolutely support your right to sleep with that dish you're marrying. It's always the quiet ones who really know how to worship a woman's body."

"Um, thank you?" I say.

"Excuse me," Seth says, in a tone of voice that says *I'm right here.*

"That's enough modernity for me." Amelie claps her hands. "I'll show you three to your rooms. Victor, stop trying to carry all those suitcases and accept you're going to have to make two trips. Sometimes there's no shortcut."

***

Dinner is as awkward as you'd expect it to be. Although the lamb is delicious, and I find out Barbie has a wicked sense of humor. Amelie wants to talk to Seth after dinner, so I head up to our bedroom alone.

The high-ceilinged room is painted white and filled with antique furniture in dark wood and silk. There's a sky-blue bedspread across a king bed big enough for two of us. Probably big enough for four of us.

I'm sleeping in the same bed as Seth.

I think about lining up a row of pillows down the bed to demark his space from mine, but it seems childish. Everything is so old, proper, and spacious, I feel exposed as I change into my pajamas. Like I'm changing in someone's living room.

The pajamas aren't anything sexy—cheap cotton shorts and a pale pink t-shirt saying *Rosé All Day* in gold glitter—but now I have a roommate, I go ahead and add a sweatshirt and fuzzy socks.

Fun fact: It's psychologically impossible to think about sex while wearing fuzzy socks.

Not that I'd be thinking about sex anyway. I crawl under the covers with my romance novel and find my place in the book. It's a sex scene.

I set the book aside, turn off the lights, and try to fall asleep. Lying in new darkness waiting for Seth to come to bed isn't particularly restful.

I change my mind about total darkness and turn on one light on Seth's side of the bed. *So he won't trip*, I tell myself.

***

The door opens softly, and I half wake, recognizing Seth's footsteps. I should let him know I'm awake, say something to ease the situation, but I don't feel like doing his emotional labor right now, so I bury my head deeper into the pillow and wait for him to get in bed.

And wait. And wait. The light goes off, and I hold my breath.

But no one gets in bed with me. I'd think he'd left the room, but I can hear his breathing. Slowing. Deepening.

I flick on my light and sit up, ready to scold him for being a weirdo who watches people while they sleep.

But he's on the far side of the room, curled up on the antique settee. It's barely two thirds the size of him, and even curled up, his limbs stick out at odd angles. He's taken off his shoes and his jacket, but other than he's fully dressed.

He blinks in the light, confused. "I thought you were asleep."

"Why aren't you wearing pajamas?" I ask.

"I was unprepared to share accommodations. I will acquire pajamas tomorrow," he says stiffly, which *hello*.

Uptight Seth Moreau said he only sleeps in his underwear. Or perhaps…

Nope, not going there.

"Um. You don't look like you fit over there."

Seth snorts, then laughs. It's the kind of laugh that's a release after a long, stressful day.

When things can't get any worse, there are two kinds of people. The kind who take it seriously because failure is a serious thing. And the kind who laugh.

I'm surprised Seth is the kind who laughs. After two years, I would have sworn he was the serious sort. But I only know him in a work context.

Seth turns his head to me, his smile crooked. Maybe there's more to him than his work.

"This is not going how I planned. You have my sincerest apologies," Seth says.

"For what?"

"For my brother. For your sleeping arrangements. For everything. It's unforgivable I dragged you into this."

I think it over, biting my lip, and for some reason, his eyes go a little unfocused.

"Here's what I think," I say. "This was a horrible idea and the two of us should never come up with a solution unsupervised again."

He groans. "You're right, I can put you on a flight back tomorrow–"

"I'm not finished. We're here now. I'm in France. You're with the aunt you love and never get to see. Neither one of us have to work for a month. So let's take it as a given we're both sorry and enjoy a month in France."

Seth studies me in the soft lamplight. "I don't think it's that easy."

"Of course it's is. At least for me. I need you to catch up to my level of irresponsibility."

There's a laugh hiding in the corner of his mouth again. I almost have him.

"If you promise not to apologize anymore this month, I'll let you have half the bed," I coax.

"You don't have to do that."

"Seth. You're sleeping in a chair."

He purses his lips virtuously. "I'm a born-again virgin. I can't share a bed with you until our wedding night."

I throw a pillow at him, and Seth cracks up laughing, so I throw a few more for good measure.

He peeks out from under the pile of pillows. "Are you sure? Because I don't want to make you uncomfortable—"

I could point out he let me sleep on him on the plane. I could point out this bed is big enough to fit me, him, and ten of his closest relatives. I could point out if he doesn't get enough sleep he'll be a complete grouch tomorrow, and I'm the one who will have to deal with it.

But he won't think any of those answers are good enough, so instead I give him the real answer.

"It's fine. I trust you."

Seth searches my face, but the settee is tiny, and he's exhausted. So he gets into bed.

The bed's so big I hardly feel a dip when he sits down. He tucks himself in until he's lying motionless, hands at his side, the covers up to his chin. He's as close to the edge of the bed as he can be without falling off.

"Comfortable?" I ask dryly.

"Very."

"You're still wearing your glasses."

He takes his glasses off and places them precisely on the bedside table.

He's so awkward I can't resist pushing his buttons a little more. "You're still wearing your belt—"

"*Enough*, Miss Smith."

I snicker and turn off the lights. And that's when I get my comeuppance because Seth is asleep almost as soon as the lights are off.

Me though? I'm wide awake, thinking about the Moreau brother next to me I can trust, and the one across the hall I can't.

***

At one a.m. I throw back the covers. I grab my book and head to the library Seth showed me earlier, planning to read until I get drowsy.

But the library is occupied.

Victor looks up from his phone. He's sitting in a giant wing-backed chair, wearing a velvet bathrobe and pajama pants.

"Finally," he says.

"What do you mean 'finally'?"

"You run away when you're nervous. You're obviously not sleeping with my brother." He takes a sip of whiskey. "Ergo, you're nervous. Ergo, you came to me."

"I did not *come to you*," I spit out.

"Fine. Have it your way." He waves a hand like he's brushing away an inconsequential detail. "But you can't deny we have things to talk about."

I cross my arms across my chest. It's a move that would work better if I weren't holding a cheesy romance novel. "What's there to talk about? You don't talk about my past, I don't talk about yours, and then we never see each other again."

He toasts me with his whiskey. "Good. I'd worried spending time with my brother might have made you…self-destructive. He's got a virtuous streak which can be so dangerous to his health."

"Don't talk about him," I bite out. Victor raises his eyebrows, and I know I've made a mistake.

"Fascinating. You care about him. People often do, you know. People like my aunt, for instance. But not people like us."

"You and I have an agreement," I say. "But that's all we have."

I turn on my heel, but Victor's soft laughter follows me down the hall.

Adrenaline coursing through me, I open the door too loudly.

Seth startles out of his sleep and falls out of bed.

"Shit, are you ok?" I rush over to him.

He rubs his head, looking confused and grumpy in his rumpled button-up shirt. I crouch, trying to help, but he waves me off.

"Why aren't you sleeping?" He yawns. "It's the middle of the night."

"I went to go read but I ran into Victor and—"

"Victor?" His sleepy gaze sharpens. "Did he say something to you?"

"…No," I say, but even half asleep, Seth can read the lie in my face.

"That does it." Seth stands abruptly.

"Wait—"

He stalks out of the room, shutting the door in my face.

Chapter Five

Seth

I storm down the hallway to Victor's room, flicking switches as I go, leaving a rude, blazing trail of light behind me.

I shove Victor's door open. "We need to fucking talk, Victor—"

"Wrong room," Barbie barks, scrambling to shove something angular and black behind her back.

I jerk the door closed. "Sorry."

"No worries," she says through the door.

I turn away before my brain catches up with my eyes, and I realize what Barbie was holding. At least, I *think*…

I rap the door. "Barbie?"

"Yes?"

"Can I come in?"

I hear footsteps, and she opens the door a sliver. "Seth honey, it's awful late."

"Yeah, that's the thing." I brace my forearm on the doorframe. "Why are you still awake, and why were you holding a gun?"

Her eyes widen, and for a second I wonder if I've miscalculated and I'm about to be shot through the door like in an American TV show.

But Barbie doesn't shoot. Instead she looks at the ceiling. "It's um… not a gun," she says in a hushed voice.

"Really? Because this is my great-aunt's home, and I don't know you at all, so—" I try to pry the door open, but Barbie is stronger than she looks. "If it's not a gun, then show me—"

"It's a sex thing, okay? Being a born-again virgin is hard."

My hold on the door loosens. That… does seem more plausible.

"Besides," Barbie says reasonably, "how would I get something like a gun through airport security?"

I'm losing my mind.

"I'm sorry, it looked so much like…"

Barbie winks. "Don't ask about my kinks and I won't ask about yours. Victor's in the library if you're looking for him."

She closes the door. I stare at it for a second. Then I set off to the library to find Victor.

It makes sense he's in the library. As kids, we'd spend a couple of weeks every summer at Aunt Amelie's. I spent my time exploring. Victor wanted the library. He wanted an escape. If he couldn't get it physically, he'd get it mentally. As soon as we were teenagers he discovered the nearby town, and I spent the next few summers cleaning up his messes, from crashed cars to insulted neighbors, to angry teen girls.

The thing with unconditional love is you don't always stop someone you should.

When I open the door, Victor's pacing restlessly, like he used to when we were boys, and he was working out a problem. Suddenly my anger is all twisted up with sadness.

Victor takes one look at my face and laughs. "My god, the little tattletale."

My jaw tightens. "She doesn't want you, and she doesn't want you bothering her. Leave her alone."

Victor pours himself another glass of whiskey. "Is that what she told you? She didn't want me? Interesting."

I fight the urge to punch him. "I'm not sixteen. I'm not falling for that."

Victor smirks. "Then why does it bother you? Admit it, she's a better fit for me than you."

I know he's stirring shit to get under my skin, but dammit, it's working. When Victor's got his well-behaved mask on, he's exactly the type of man Darcy would fall for. He fakes the kind of artsy charm she genuinely has, and his flakiness looks like spontaneity until you know better.

"Tell you what," Victor says. "Let's swap. You take Barbie, I'll take delicious Darcy. What's one fake fiancée compared to another?"

I grab his shirt and he stumbles, his whiskey sloshing onto the carpet.

"Leave. Darcy. Alone. Do you understand me?"

Victor raises an eyebrow. "My, my. You haven't gotten this angry since I sicced the FBI on you."

My hands tighten in his shirt as I lift him. "I said, do you understand me?"

Something flickers in Victor's eyes. In another man, I'd think it was fear. He buries it with an eye roll. "Fine, yes, I understand you."

I release him, and Victor rubs his neck like the dramatic fuck he is.

I turn to go.

"Don't you want to know what Darcy and I were discussing? What we have in common she can't talk to you about?"

Yes.

But I say, "You're drunk. Drink some water and go to bed." I leave him in the library, surrounded by books he'll never read and alcohol that will be gone by dawn.

When I slide back into bed, Darcy's breathing is slow and deep.

She's asleep.

I shift to face her across the vast bed. "He won't bother you anymore." My voice is so low and soft *I* almost can't hear it. "I promise."

I'm floating somewhere on the edge of sleep and waking, when I dream Darcy whispers, "I know."

***

The room is filled with the slow, easy glow of morning, and I'm breathing in something fresh, lemony, and warm. One of my arms pricks with pins and needles, weighed down by something heavy. But I don't care because there's a delightful scent. I follow it and am rewarded when hair soft as silk slides over my skin.

She sighs, and I pull her closer to me on instinct.

Wait. Shit. My eyes fly open.

I'm tangled up in Darcy. I'm curled around her, my knees bumping up against the back of hers, my arm wrapped around her waist. I try to extract myself, but her arm is holding mine, and my other arm is pinned under her head.

Darcy snores. At least she's a heavy sleeper.

I try to pull my arm away, but her grip tightens. So I focus on sliding my other arm out from under her head, inch by torturous inch.

This is fine. It's Jenga. Super stressful, inconveniently sexual Jenga. My arm is almost all the way out from under her head when Darcy rolls to face me.

My breath catches.

I see Darcy every day.

But for some reason, right now, with her breathing deep, and her dark lashes splayed across her full cheeks, I'm back on that sidewalk two years ago, staring at a pretty, vibrant girl who blasted into my life like a gale of fresh air, and was about to blast on out again if I didn't think of something to say, fast.

Except the thing that fell out of my mouth was a dumb joke about a job, and she took me seriously. Finding a good assistant is way harder than finding a date.

The pretty girl on the sidewalk is a ghost of a memory compared to the full force of Darcy Smith, my real-life coworker.

Victor would have known what to say.

Granted, he would have broken her heart or stolen her wallet. But he would have known what to say.

Darcy nestles closer, her face even with mine on the pillow, and I know I should back up, get off the bed, there is no reason for my arm to still be resting on the warm, solid curve of her waist, but I lie there, staring, while my traitorous brain thinks "what if."

It's disorienting. Like being at an optometrist when they're showing you two different letters, both blurry and straining your eyes in different ways, and you're supposed to pick the correct one, or the way you see the world will be a little wrong forever.

I pull my hand from Darcy's waist. I made my choice.

Her eyes fly open.

I scramble back and fall off the bed. Again.

I blink up at the ceiling, dizzy. I suppose it's some comfort she invaded *my* side of the bed.

Darcy peeks over the edge, her brown curls spilling around her face. She looks like a hot mess of an angel, and I close my eyes, trying desperately to think work thoughts.

Emails. Office supplies. Paper cuts.

"… Do I want to know?" Darcy asks.

"Not really," I say without opening my eyes.

There's a rap on the door.

"Breakfast is ready when you are," Amelie calls gaily.

"Thank you," Darcy returns, sounding positively chipper.

I sit up, rubbing the back of my head. I need to get us separate rooms. Sharing a bed with Darcy Smith is hazardous to my health.

***

Victor and I face off at the breakfast table like American football players waiting for the whistle to blow. Or the guy to yell hike, or however American football starts.

Darcy sits to my right, across from Barbie. Aunt Amelie presides at the head, master of all.

"So," Amelie says. "Did everyone sleep well?"

"I slept wonderfully." Victor smirks at me. "Seth?"

"Like a baby."

Darcy sips her coffee out of a fine porcelain cup and looks at the ceiling.

"Hmm. And you, Barbie?" Amelie inquires.

"In bed by nine, saying my prayers, ma'am."

I snort, and Darcy kicks me under the table.

"And you, Amelie?" Darcy asks.

"Horribly. There was shouting, and pacing, and door slamming, and a huge thump like someone was falling out of bed. I could have sworn it was you all, but since you all were apparently sound asleep…"

Victor takes Amelie's hand soothingly. "You must have imagined it. An old house like this when you're living alone? It could play tricks on anyone."

The absolute prick. I open my mouth to tell Amelie the truth, but Darcy gives a slight shake of her head. Below the table, where the others can't see, she holds up her hand, motioning me to slow down. Like I do with our gallery director when he's jumping in instead of reading the client.

I look over at Amelie. Sure enough, she's immune to Victor's steering. Her gaze is icy as she looks him up and down. Victor withdraws his hand, shrinking in his seat.

"I think what we meant," Darcy says, "is we slept well enough, considering the jet lag. Travel can be stressful."

"Yes, especially with all the lying," Amelie says.

I choke on my coffee. "Lying? No one's lying. I'm not—"

"Flying, dear," Darcy says, and takes my hand. Her fingers thread through my mine, squeezing in a *shut up, you idiot* signal. "She said flying."

I look at Amelie, who holds my gaze steadily.

Yeah, she didn't say "flying."

Amelie raises an eyebrow and rips off a piece of croissant. "Why on earth would you think I said lying? Unless one of you boys has something to tell me?"

I'm tempted to blurt the truth. But when I look at Victor, I can't help but think of everything I've trusted him with over the years: secrets, money, art, relationships. *Everything* has been broken. He even managed to break us, and I didn't even realize I'd trusted him with it.

I'm not letting him break the place Amelie has loved her whole life.

When I look at Amelie, my voice is firm. "No. Nothing to tell."

"In that case, I have a brilliant idea. Why don't you all get married here, at the end of the month?"

Darcy bangs her coffee cup on the saucer. Barbie's eyes go wide.

Victor leans back in his chair. "That's very romantic of you, Aunt Amelie. But weddings take time."

"Nonsense. Last night you all said you wanted simple weddings. Something simple at the end of the month is no problem."

"Darcy's and Barbie's families wouldn't have enough warning. And we don't know if Mom and Dad can get the time off," I argue.

"Your parents are in Birmingham. Barely a four-hour flight. They can clear one weekend for the wedding of both their sons." She turns to Darcy and Barbie. "And girls, I am happy to fly out anyone you want. As a gift."

Darcy looks pale. "Completely unnecessary."

"Nope. Nope, nope, nope," Barbie says at the same time.

I try to regain control of the conversation. "Why do you want it so soon, Amelie?"

"I want to be around for it. And at my age…" She tries to look old and frail, but it's not working.

"No," Victor says.

"Why not?" Amelie looks from Victor to me. "Unless you don't really intend to get married and you've dragged these poor women across an ocean purely for my benefit?"

"Because Darcy and I think *our* wedding should be when *we* want it, does not make what we have together a lie." I glance over at Darcy. What was it she said about lying? *You have to be thinking about the story behind what you're saying.*

I gaze at Darcy and think of all the ways she's threaded into my daily life. The way she makes my workdays more complicated, but she makes them better too, with her laughter and her company and the way she sees the world. The way the gallery has been a brighter, faster place since she blew in and took over.

"I can't imagine my life without her," I say, utterly sincere.

Darcy's smile is surprised and luminous. Like when a spring breeze blows through a room, stirring everything up and bringing with it the scent of fresh, wild things. My pulse quickens.

"Barbie and I will get married at the end of the month," Victor says.

My gaze snaps to his.

Victor leans toward me. "Talk is cheap. What is it you're always saying to me? 'Intentions don't matter, actions do.'"

He turns to Amelie, taking Barbie's hand almost as an afterthought. "If you want a wedding at the end of the month, I'll give you one."

And then he says the thing he's been saying all our lives. The thing I believed, every time until that last, worst time: "You can count on me."

My blood boils. I drop Darcy's hand.

"We'll do it, too," I say. "We'll get married here, at the end of the month."

"*Seth,*" Darcy hisses.

"Are you sure?" Amelie asks, and for some reason, she's not including Victor in the question. Only me.

"Yes," I say. "I'm sure."

Darcy throws down her napkin. "Excuse me." Her chair scrapes the floor loudly as she shoves away from the table and storms out.

Victor smirks. "Uh-oh. Trouble in paradise."

"Look who's talking," Barbie mutters.

I stand. "Excuse me, Amelie."

She stops me with a hand on my arm. "Be careful there, Seth. She's not one you want to lose."

Chapter Six

Darcy Sherwood

I need air. This has gotten way out of control.

It's like I don't recognize Seth anymore. I had to convince him to lie to Amelie in the first place. Now he's lying so well *I* almost believe him.

My mind flashes to his eyes, clear and sincere, as he said *I can't imagine my life without her.* Now he announces we're getting married?

I burst out a side door and onto the back terrace overlooking a massive hedge maze to the right and scattered wildflowers to the left. I inhale sharply, letting the cold air pierce my chest. It's hard not to feel like my past is finally catching up with me. First Victor, now this.

The door opens, and without turning around, I know it's Seth. He stops at least three feet behind me. Always leaving a careful distance.

"Darcy, I—"

"I can't get married, Seth."

"It's not a marriage, only a wedding. If we don't file the paperwork—"

"I'm already married."

I turn to face him. He looks like he's been socked in the jaw.

I wrap my arms around myself like I'm trying to shield myself from his judgment. Or maybe from all the bad decisions I've made.

Seth slumps against the stone wall of the chateau, head tilted back to the sky. He closes his eyes and asks, voice strained, "Do you love him?"

"No."

He looks at me. "Then why? How long? Why didn't you tell me? Why did you suggest we—" He cuts himself off with a futile hand gesture.

I take a deep breath. "It was shortly after I met you. He needed to qualify for more financial aid for grad school. I needed a new last name. There were people I knew who weren't...good people. I needed a fresh start." I shrug. "It seemed like a good idea at the time."

"You're still married."

"He graduates in two months. We're getting the divorce then. I already marked the time I'm taking off to go down to the courthouse on the office calendar. I...you know, marked it as a dentist appointment."

Seth gives a broken laugh. "Of course you did."

"You should have checked with me before you announced we're getting married."

He jabs a finger at me. "I'm not the one who came up with this engagement idea."

"You're the one who wanted to use me as the fiancée."

"You're the one who said yes."

"Because you said *please,* you asshole." I throw my hands in the air. "Why is this a conversation? Go tell Amelie we can't get married. This is not my problem."

Seth starts to argue, but I turn on my heel and stomp down the terrace steps and into the first row of towering hedges, which open up before me. I'm already drowning in my emotions. I don't have room for his.

For a while it's peaceful, with only the sound of my footsteps in the wet grass, and the gentle morning calls of the neighborhood birds. I breathe in the quiet, trying to let it soak into my skin.

Then I hear the quick, confident stride of Seth's footsteps on the other side of the hedge.

He's coming after me. And I don't want to deal with him. It's immature, but I don't. Seth will be logical. Or worse, he'll be kind.

I run deeper into the maze. The icy air settles in my lungs like another thing to carry. I lose track of the turns. Seth calls my name, but I keep running.

His steps pick up. He's jogging toward me. But I'm too many turns ahead of him.

"Darcy, please talk to me. This is ridiculous."

Ah yes. The phrase every woman loves to hear from her man.

Not that Seth's my man. I run faster. I turn too fast in a patch of mud and shriek when my legs go sliding to the side, out from under me. My palms sting as they hit the ground.

"Darcy! Darcy, are you ok?" Seth calls from a few hedges away.

"I'm fine," I say.

"Stay there."

The hedges rustle and shake. I hear a branch snap, and he swears.

Seth's spectacled face peeks out over the top of the hedge. He's streaked in dirt, and his clothes are a rumpled mess, but he's surprisingly agile as he swings over to my side of the hedge and drops to the ground.

Who is this man and what has he done with Office Seth?

He crouches down next to me. "Anything hurt?"

"Only my pride. You climb hedges?"

"What? Oh, all the neighborhood kids climbed these," he says, like it's nothing to scale six feet of shrubbery in designer slacks. He stands and offers me a hand.

I hesitate. "I'm still mad at you."

"I gathered. But you can be mad at me standing up, instead of sitting in the mud."

I glower, but I let him pull me up.

He's stronger than I expect, and I end up stumbling too close. I catch myself against Seth's chest. When his heart speeds up, I feel it against my fingertips.

I drop my hands and back away. It's because he was running. Because he climbed a fucking hedge. Because we're in the middle of a fight.

It doesn't have anything to do with me.

Like the way my heart is racing has nothing to do with him.

We stare at each other. In the background, two birds are trading songs, trying to find each other.

Abruptly, Seth starts pacing. He's in problem-solving mode.

Normally I'd wait patiently for him to stop pacing and present his solution. I almost do it again, out of habit.

But this isn't Seth's gallery. It's my life. "To be clear, you're trying to come up with a way to tell Amelie we aren't getting married at the end of the month, right?"

He pivots to face me. "Hear me out. I wasn't going to file the paperwork anyway. And if it's not legal, it wouldn't conflict with your marriage."

"So *not* the point."

He rubs his temples. "Then what is? You're clearly ok using a fake marriage to achieve your ends. What's the difference?"

"Are you fucking serious?"

He shrugs, clearly frustrated.

"The difference was it was the only way I could think of to get a thing I needed."

"Well, this is the only way *I* can think of to get something *I* need. I can't let Victor destroy—"

"But what about me? I know I'm not the most romantic person in the world. It's not like I'm expecting some man to go down on bended knee with candles and rose petals. But I would like to get married someday, for real, and each time I use it like it's nothing... Helping you lie about being engaged over FaceTime is one thing. This is too much."

Seth starts pacing again. He stops, makes a face, then nods. Like he's doing math in his head. He turns back to me. For some reason, it feels different than before. There's a surface-level, shiny confidence to him, like how he is with a client.

"Right then. How much would it take, Darcy?"

"What?" I ask, stunned.

"You said you only did this before because it benefited you. How much would I have to pay for this to help you, too?"

I stare at Seth. We bicker all the time. But in two years of working with him, this is the first time I've felt like we're truly fighting each other. Like I got kicked off his team and turned into his rival in one fell swoop.

Fury and hurt sits in my stomach. If he's going to treat me like a client, then I'm going to be the most fucking obnoxious client there is.

"You always say never negotiate against yourself. How much are you willing to pay?" I dare.

"Half a million dollars."

"*What?*" I yelp. "You're fucking *kidding* me."

Seth crosses his arms, defensive. "I'm not being reckless. I can make more money. I can't replace my family's heritage. And you're my only option, which means you have the power. So half a million dollars."

"You can find another fiancée—"

"Amelie's not going to believe I asked two women to marry me in one year. It's you, or no one."

I'm overwhelmed. Both at the idea of half a million dollars, and because...

I shake my head. "I don't have the power. You can fire me if I say no."

"I... I don't even know where to start unpacking that one."

"Well, try."

Seth shoots me a look, then starts ticking off points on his fingers. "One: This is a separate proposition from your job. Your choice has no effect on your excellent work as an assistant, except if you take the half-million, you'd have no reason to work for me anymore."

"One," I counter. "Power dynamics exist, and to pretend they don't is naive and foolish."

"Two: Only an asshole would take advantage of that power dynamic," he continues.

"Two: You're taking advantage of it right now by trying to talk over me—"

"Three: I know for a fact at least two other galleries have tried to poach you since the Cohen show. I assume there will be others. I try to give my employees good jobs. But it's only a job, and you have other options."

I shake my head. "It's not just a job."

"Why? What makes this job so special you're more worried about losing it than getting half a million dollars?"

You. I like working with you.

The thought catches me off guard. I've been telling myself I don't want to leave my life at the gallery. I like the people I work with, the friends I go out for drinks with, the routines I have with my favorite coffee shop, and my favorite sandwich place. I love the moment most afternoons in the gallery when the office seems to fall silent and it's only me, a doable checklist, and late afternoon sunlight falling in squares of gold on the floor.

But the truth is, I don't want to leave Seth. What started as me hiding from my past and him being a workaholic has turned into the closest friendship I have. It would have been smart to keep my boundaries up. But I was lonely. And sometimes, late at night, I thought Seth might be lonely too.

My whole life has been some version of "try harder, you're not good enough." Seth makes things different. He assumes I can handle it, and if not, the problem is the task, not me. I've never had a boss think I'm already good enough.

"Come on, Darcy," Seth says, his voice coaxing. "It's half a million. What would you do with half a million dollars? Buy your dream home? Travel the world? Finish art school? You could be so much more."

I flinch. "Why can't things stay the way they are? You're good at running a gallery. I'm good at running you."

"Exactly. No challenge. It's not like you were going to stick around and be just my administrative assistant forever," Seth says dismissively, and it feels like a slap in the face.

Like there's something wrong with me if I want to stay "just" his assistant.

"I've made a good life for myself," I hiss. "And you have no idea how hard it was. So stop trying to make me unhappy with my life because you're trapped in yours."

I turn to leave the maze, but I can't remember which way is out. The hedges rise around me like barbed wire and every exit looks wrong.

"The path on the right," Seth says unhappily.

I take it, and I don't look back.

***

I creep back into the house, but I shouldn't have worried. Everyone is gone from the breakfast room.

There's a surprising amount of light for a place so old. Amelie has filled the halls with delicate mirrors and gorgeous art, like windows to another world.

I peek into one enchanting room after another. It's a huge house for one woman, even one whose personality is as big as Amelie's. It's easy to imagine why she would have enjoyed hosting her nephews every summer.

I picture the Moreau men as boys. Seth, young and serious, with perpetually crooked glasses. Victor, bright and vivacious, trying to get away with everything under the sun.

I think of all the layers of memories Seth must have here. How careful he is with Amelie, how obviously he loves her. It must have pressed every button Seth had to watch Victor patronize and belittle Amelie at breakfast.

I wrap my arms around myself as I walk, not sure why my eyes sting. Of course Seth would do anything to protect this place. It's my bad luck that in trying to save it, he's ripping away every security blanket I have. Victor knows my new name. Seth doesn't care if we stop working together. He doesn't think I'm enough.

I mean, he thinks I can be bought with half a million dollars, so props to him for not thinking I'm cheap. I rub my hands over my face like I can wipe the embarrassment and fear and grief away.

I should have taken one of those other gallery job offers.

Of course, if I'd done that, I would have lived my whole life without ever seeing bar-fight Seth. Hedge-climbing Seth. Struggling-with-suitcases Seth. Falling-out-of-bed-because-he's-trying-to-be-a-gentleman Seth.

Why did he have to say 'Please'?

Down the hall, I hear classical music with quick, driving, adventurous violins and the soft sounds of a woman talking.

As I get closer, I catch the tangy, chemical scent of wet paint, and I'm hit with a heartache so deep I hesitate in the doorway, gripping the door frame for support.

Amelie's perched on a stool in an old, paint-covered sweater, in front of a partially finished canvas. She's got a paintbrush in one hand, her cell phone in the other. She's laughing into the phone, her voice soft and husky.

"Belle, darling, you know I miss you too. But this isn't the right time for you to meet them. They're being little shits right now, and I want you to love them as much as I do…Yes… Belle! You dirty girl. Fine, yes, lunch… No, not today. Tomorrow… *Je t'aime.*"

Amelie laughs softly as she hangs up. When she twists around to set her phone on a nearby table, her cheeks are flushed and girlish.

She spots me and nearly drops her phone. "Oh."

"I didn't mean to overhear, I smelled the paint and…" I trail off. I realize I am deeply weird to say *I smelled the paint* the way other people say *I smelled the chocolate chip cookies.*

But Amelie's eyes brighten. "Oh, you're an artist. Seth didn't tell me."

"Was. A long time ago. I… I don't anymore." I spent more years forging for Victor than I did working on my own stuff in art school. And the ugly secret is, it was *fun.* Losing myself in Monet's gardens, in Van Gogh's nights. I loved disappearing into beautiful paintings without stopping to think about the consequences of what I was doing. Now when I look at a paintbrush, all I can see are the consequences.

I realize I'm twisting Seth's engagement ring.

Amelie brushes off my words with an elegant hand. "There is no *was* for artists. You are merely lying dormant."

What are she and Seth doing to me? I'm happy with my life. *I'm happy.*

Amelie turns back to her canvas. "Be a dear and set up the other easel, in front of this window?"

I can't exactly say no, so I do it, feeling a little click of satisfaction when it locks into place.

"And the blank canvas in the corner—if you could put it on the easel? They're a bit unwieldy for me."

I add the canvas, loving the way it all looks. There's something about a blank canvas. Beautiful, terrifying, wonderful. If I were going to make a modern art piece, it would be a blank canvas. And I'd call it *Possibility.*

I turn to go.

Amelie passes me a palette, and some tubes of paint, without taking her eyes off the painting she's currently working on. "Squeeze some onto the palette, would you? The weather is getting my arthritis today."

Ok, this is getting excessive. What's she going to do, paint two pieces at once? The paint will dry on this palette before she finishes what's on her current one. But I do as she asks. I'm looking for a place to set down the palette when she hands me a brush.

I blink. I look at the canvas I set up, and the paint I squeezed.

"There's a spare paint shirt in the corner," she says, as she leans into her work.

"Amelie…"

She turns on her stool to look at me. "Unless you can honestly say you don't want to. But I think you want to."

I look at the blank canvas, which has edged from the wondrous end of the spectrum over to terrifying. "I… I don't want to waste your art supplies."

Amelie tsks. "True wealth is being able to buy as many art supplies as you want."

I laugh, and she smiles.

"Go on then," Amelie says. "Paint me something to remember you by."

I don't know if that's her way of saying she knows Seth and I are lying, or if she doesn't think the marriage will last, or if she doesn't expect me to visit again anytime soon.

But the reminder I'm never coming back—that I'll never see her, or this room, or this canvas again—is oddly freeing.

What the hell. I'm on vacation. Sort of. People do crazy things on vacation.

I take a deep breath. Stare at the canvas. Feel the delicate, perfect weight of the brush in my hand. *No consequences*, I tell myself.

The vast white expanse stares back at me.

A memory comes back to me, of my instructor berating me for not having my own voice. Asking why all my recent paintings looked like the knockoff works of dead men. And the realization slowly rising, until I'm drowning in fear, that I don't have a voice anymore. I'm a forger. Nothing more. I've gotten too good at hiding. No one will ever find me again. I can't even find myself.

Not good enough.

Amelie reaches out and paints a jagged slash of green across the center of my canvas.

"Hey—"

"Fix it."

"But—"

"Stop hyperventilating. Fix it." She adds, "If it's good, I'll let you pick the music next time."

Next time. This doesn't have to be the last time I hold a brush. I'm not painting for a grade. Or for a client. I'm not even painting for my reputation.

No, the only stakes I'm painting for is who gets to choose the radio station.

I stare at the green, and the deep, cool weight of it makes me think of the hedges in the maze. How they almost seemed to block out the sky when I was down on the ground.

I lean around my canvas to look out the window. The hedges aren't particularly interesting from here, but they're visible enough I can use them for a reference. They don't feel so threatening anymore now I'm out of the maze with a brush in my hand.

I look over at Amelie. There's a smile hiding in the corner of her mouth again. She thinks I can do it.

Maybe my problem wasn't realizing art had consequences. It was forgetting some of those consequences could be good.

"You're on," I say, and dip my brush in blue.

Chapter Seven

Seth

After Darcy leaves, I head to the heart of the maze. Darcy clearly doesn't want me to follow her. We've never fought like that.

My feet know the way like I'm seventeen again. Moody, out of place, searching for a place to hide.

I step into the center, a roughly circular patch of grass. There's an old, magnificent orange tree, surrounded by a bed of lavender. When I was a kid, I'd lie in the lavender for hours until my heart calmed down.

I hesitate at the edge of the circle. I don't feel like I have the right to be somewhere this peaceful.

Just an administrative assistant. Way to fuck that one up.

I can't believe she's married. I can't believe anyone would ask Darcy to marry them for a break in tuition. Fuck, she's worth so much more than that.

Granted, I'm trying to do the same thing, so glass houses, I suppose.

Except it doesn't *feel* the same. I'm introducing her to my family. I'm showing her France. I sure as hell wouldn't let some other man pretend to be her fiancé. This Smith man is a fucking idiot.

Who are these people Darcy's trying to get away from? People so bad she felt she had to change her name? The back of my neck prickles at the thought of Darcy in danger and I get a sudden urge to go back into the house, to make sure she's ok.

Which is ridiculous. There's no one in Amelie's chateau Darcy needs to hide from.

Feeling antsy, I start walking the perimeter of the circle.

I should be planning how to convince Darcy to fake a wedding with me at the end of the month. Or how to break it to Amelie there won't be a wedding.

But all I can think of is the look on Darcy's face. Did she really plan on being my administrative assistant forever?

Normally when people stay in a career they're comfortable with, it's because it lets them focus on other areas of their lives. Friends, family, hobbies, vacation. But Darcy's as much of a workaholic as me. She loves art museums and thrift stores, and she has plenty of friends she meets for drinks. But they're not the kind of friends you go on vacation with or rearrange your schedule for. Hell, when she had to get her appendix out, I was the one who took her to and from the hospital.

You don't work that hard unless you're working toward something. I'd promote her, except she'd never seemed interested in anything else at the gallery.

I always figured she'd leave. But I *was* telling the truth at breakfast. I can't imagine my life without her.

How can both of those things be true? What did I think would happen when she—

Oh God.

I stumble to a halt.

Deep in the back of my mind, where you store the thoughts and plans you know it's wrong to have, is my answer.

Without ever verbalizing it, even to myself, I was planning on courting Darcy when she left. And I was planning on her saying yes.

I stare ahead in horror, wondering if this is why I haven't clicked with anyone I've gone out with in the last few years.

There was a part of me, deep down, waiting for Darcy.

Meanwhile, she's fucking married. She's perfectly content to go on with our platonic, professional relationship until we retire.

Fuck. Fuck, fuck, fuck, fuck, fuuuuuuck.

I sit down in the lavender and bury my head in my hands. I can't fake-marry her when I've been carrying *that* torch inside of me.

I stand. I'll tell Amelie there was a work emergency. She said I had a year. I'll come up with something, anything, that does *not* involve bribing Darcy into playing fiancée with me.

Because it's one thing when we both know the score: professional, platonic, mutually beneficial.

When I'm out here in unrequited-interest land? Lusting after my employee?

Power dynamics exist, and to pretend they don't is naive and foolish.

She'd hate me if she knew. Well, maybe not hate. But she'd think less of me. The thought of Darcy being disappointed in me hurts like a breakup you *know* is coming but are still desperately trying to avert.

I can't lose her. I have to get us out of here, back home, and back to normal. Hopefully, it's not too late.

***

I search for Amelie until I hear her old staticky radio and realize she's in her studio.

"Amelie, there's been a work thing, we have to leave early..." I round the corner, and the words die in my mouth.

Darcy's sitting next to Amelie, at an easel of her own. She's painting. To be more precise, she's painting me.

At least, part of me. It's a fairly sedate, traditional landscape of the maze.

Except I'm popping over the top of the hedge, glasses askew. It's only my hands, and the top half of my face, but I can tell it's me.

Her brushstrokes are loose, her colors rich and warm.

Darcy looks back at me, and there's a light in her face I've never seen. Her smile has this deep, liquid quality, like good red wine on a summer day. A brilliant swipe of cerulean on her cheek sets off her gray eyes.

"...You were saying?" Amelie asks me, and I yank my eyes from Darcy.

"There's been a, uh, work thing. I'm sorry, but we have to leave early."

"No we don't," Darcy says.

"What?" Amelie says.

"What?" I say.

Darcy turns to Amelie. "He's trying to cover for me. I wasn't sure I wanted to get married at the end of the month—it's so soon, you know?—but I've thought about it, and why not? It matters so much to you and Seth."

"Yes, but it should matter to you too," I cut in. I try desperately to signal her to stop.

Darcy smiles at me, and there's something sad and knowing and wicked in her smile.

"As long as you're there," Darcy coos, "I'll have everything I need."

Everything in me tightens in response. God help me.

Amelie claps her hands in glee, sending paint splattering from her brush. "Oh, wonderful. I'll get the wedding planning binder."

"Binder?" I ask, but Amelie is already flying from the room, leaving me alone with Darcy.

Darcy, who I have apparently been subconsciously lusting after for years.

She bites her lip, and my eyes flicker to her lush mouth like they always do.

Ok, maybe it hasn't been *that* subconscious.

"The half a million is still on the table, right?" she asks.

I shake my head. "Darcy, I never should have—"

"Because I need to stop working for you."

My heart stops.

Maybe she realized the same thing as me. Maybe there's a reason she's not in a relationship either.

Darcy sets down her paintbrush carefully. "We blew up a perfectly good professional relationship with this trip."

You have no idea. I nod, my mouth dry.

"As much as we wish we could go back, we can't," she says. "I need to stop caring so much about what you think. Which means I need to stop working for you. Besides, there are…other factors."

"Darcy, I'm so sorry."

She shrugs. "It's time I move on. And as long as we're blowing this thing up, let's blow it up in style. One customized fake marriage for you. One half-a-million-dollar paycheck for me. Deal?"

She holds out a hand streaked in paint. All the colors of the rainbow, dancing on her palm.

My heart is pounding. I should say no. I've got feelings for her. She doesn't for me. This is so, so wrong.

But she wants the half a million dollars. And if she's quitting, she's not my employee anymore. And if I keep my behavior exactly the same, she never has to know…

Power dynamics exist.

Slowly, I nod. "Ok. But I'm putting the money in escrow. At the end of the month, if Amelie's got a photo of you and me in front of an officiant, you get the money. No matter what else happens this month. It's yours."

"Seth, I trust you–"

I shake my head. "If we're going to do this, I want it to be professional. More than professional. Equal."

She studies me, and I find myself shifting nervously. Adjusting my glasses. Waiting under her vivid, uncompromising stare to hear what Darcy Smith thinks.

Except she's not Darcy Smith is she? Not really. She's Darcy… someone I don't know at all.

"All right," she says. "Equal." We shake.

Her grip is strong, firm, and covered in wet paint.

"Oh shit. Here." She takes the edge of her paint shirt and, after tugging me close, uses it to wipe my hand.

I'm near enough to feel her warmth and breathe in her shampoo. In a month she'll be gone from my life.

"Am I interrupting something?" Amelie asks from the doorway, and we spring apart.

"I just… paint… shirt," I blurt like an idiot.

"Yes, I'm sure there was," Amelie says archly. Then she grins like a kid on Christmas and holds up a rather threatening binder.

"So," she says. "Let's talk wedding details."

Chapter Eight

Darcy

Once I quit my job and decide I'm getting fake-married to my ex-boss for half a million dollars, the day is relatively uneventful. Amelie goes through the binder with a zealous, bordering on malicious, look in her eye for hours before Barbie has the misfortune to wander in. Amelie pounces on Barbie, but Barbie is not about to suffer alone and drags Victor into it.

Which leaves us all in the parlor planning our double wedding.

One big happy family.

I'm so exhausted by the time Seth and I head up to our bedroom, I almost don't notice the tension radiating off him.

You'd think me officially not working for him would make Mr. Upright & Proper relax about the whole room-sharing thing. If anything, it's made him worse.

He still hasn't gotten pajamas, so the only way I know he's ready for bed is when he brushes his teeth and takes off his wing-tipped shoes.

Instead of getting into bed, he takes his pillow and a throw blanket off the settee. "I'm sleeping in one of the rooms being remodeled. I'll set an alarm and be back down before Amelie invites everyone down to breakfast."

I frown. "Aren't those rooms under construction?"

"They're... a little open to the elements. Technically. But it's fine. There's a tarp. And I like sleeping in a cold room."

Given the frigid temperature he keeps the office at, I believe him.

When Seth leaves, it's a relief to finally, finally be alone. I sink down into the covers.

This day. Hell, this week.

It's all gone so fast. But I know I made the right decision, to quit. I forgot how painting clears out space for me to think.

I can't work for someone who thinks I'm not enough. Not when I think he's so much more than enough. And working for Seth puts me way too close to Victor.

It would be one thing if I didn't have any other options. But half a million dollars? That gives me a lot of options.

I roll over onto my side. Maybe it's for the best Seth said what he said. It will make it sting less when I disappear again to hide from Victor.

At least that's what I tell myself as I fall asleep in the cold, giant bed.

***

I wake up to a crack of lightning. The wind is howling, and rain lashes the window. It's like something out of an old movie. Trapped in a giant house with a bunch of suspects and one criminal. I reach blindly for Seth wanting the reassurance of simple human warmth, but all I find are empty sheets. I turn to see if the storm woke him up too, and then I remember.

I'm alone. Seth's upstairs. In a room that is, quote, "a little open to the elements."

I pull up another blanket, not because I need the warmth, but because I need the comforting weight of heavy wool.

Seth's probably fine. He was probably exaggerating about the room.

Thunder booms, and I jump. The wind is so strong the windows are rattling.

Seth doesn't exaggerate. I know it like I know water is wet and this room is cold as ice.

I shiver as I throw back the covers. I put on my slippers and switch my phone to flashlight mode.

I'll make sure he's fine, I tell myself.

The old wood creaks under my feet as I creep through the dark halls. I find a small spiral staircase (probably a servant's staircase at one point) and clutch the railing as I slowly make my way up. I don't want to plunge to my death in an ancient French chateau.

When I get to the next floor, my flashlight shows tarps and paint cans competing for space with bedroom furniture piled in the hall.

The first few doors are open, and when I look inside, it's clear why Seth didn't pick those. There's no furniture, and the rooms smell of wet paint.

I knock on the first closed door. "Seth?"

There's no answer. Slowly, I turn the doorknob and peer into the blackness.

I'm hit with a vicious slap of cold air. This room has furniture and no paint, but the window panes are being replaced. The tarp supposed to be covering the window flaps madly in the breeze.

I shine my flashlight on the bed, breathing a sigh of relief when Seth's not there.

He's an idiot, but he's not *that* much of an idiot.

I turn to leave when my flashlight catches an old leather couch scooted in the corner, far away from the window. There's a large bundle of blankets on the couch.

A bundle that's shivering.

"Seth," I bark, and he sits up, disoriented. He blinks in the glare of my phone.

"Darcy? Is something wrong? Do you need he-he-help..." He clamps his jaw shut, but it's too late.

His teeth are literally chattering.

"That's it. You're coming with me, Moreau." I march over to him. "I don't care you don't like having a roomie. If every college freshman can get over it, you can too."

"That's not why-y-y-y..."

"Get your ass downstairs."

He tucks his chin and does his best to burrow into blankets too short for him. "No."

I'd like to stand here and get to the root of whatever bed-sharing neurosis he has, but *my* teeth are starting to chatter, so I rip the blanket off him.

"*Why?*" Seth howls, curling into a half-asleep, frozen ball.

I grab him by the collar and yank him up off the couch and down to my level in one fluid motion. "Come on, Moreau. We're going downstairs where you are going to sleep in a bed, with windows that close, like a normal person."

He blinks. "But I told you I'd get us different rooms. I promised."

That's why he's freezing his ass off up here?

He glances back at the couch, and I can see the noble-idiot in him rising again.

"There are things worth getting hypothermia over," I say sternly. "My virtue is not one of them. Is yours?"

He hesitates. Then he swears. "No. Shit no. It's freezing in here. I can't feel my toes, Darcy."

"Then let's go downstairs, Seth."

He nods eagerly, then abruptly turns back to the window. "We should fix the tarp. So the water doesn't get in."

"Why-y-y-y?" I whine. This time my teeth are the ones chattering.

"I couldn't do it by myself. But now you're here. Please."

I groan and stomp to the window.

Seth Moreau and his fucking "pleases." I bet he'd win every argument with a girlfriend that way if he ever got around to having a girlfriend. He'd say *please* with those virtuous puppy dog eyes, and she'd find herself doing ridiculous things like wrestling a tarp in a freak storm in a foreign country while pretending to be engaged.

By the time we catch both ends of the tarp and get it secured, we're drenched and shivering.

"Should we-e-e-e... Ch-ch-check the other r-oo-oo-ooms?" I ask.

"Hell no. I'm not a saint."

Could have fooled me.

He grabs my hand and tows me out of the room before anything else can go wrong.

I nearly weep for joy when we successfully make it back to our room. Seth hits the light switch, and we're bathed in cheerful, normal light instead of weird spooky darkness. My clothes are drenched, so I grab some sweats and duck into the bathroom to change.

When I come out, Seth's peeling off his sodden shirt, his back to me as he tosses the white fabric aside.

Oh. *Oh.*

I can see now why it was so easy for him to climb the hedge. I assumed Seth was strong, but... My eyes trace the lean muscles of his back as he bends to shuck his pants.

Gray boxer briefs, for anyone at home wondering.

Stop it, I scold myself. *He's your boss.*

A traitorous thought creeps into my head: *He's not your boss anymore.*

Maybe it's the adrenaline of fighting the storm, but I feel my heart pounding. My pulse thickening.

Maybe...

He turns, catches sight of me, and nearly trips stepping out of his pants. "Jesus. I didn't hear you. I'm not—I was trying to change while you were in the bathroom..." He grabs blindly for a pair of pants and yanks them on.

He grabs another dress shirt and starts buttoning. I watch all his warm skin disappear behind designer tailoring. All this time, Seth looked like *that*?

He glances up and catches me staring. "Um. Earth to Darcy."

Shit. Are my cheeks hot? They feel hot.

Wait, he's blushing too. Fuck, I've made him uncomfortable.

"I'm sorry, I … I thought you wore undershirts," I trail off lamely. Which is true (as I discovered one particularly bad time when I dumped coffee on him), but not why I'm staring.

"You said they were old-fashioned," Seth says, then immediately presses his lips tightly together, like he wishes he could take that sentence back.

Seth changed what underwear he wears because of something I said?

Not that undershirts are underwear. Exactly. It's not like if he said he liked women in thongs, and I started wearing thongs. It's like if he said he liked women who didn't wear camisoles, and then I... stopped.

I shift, feeling suddenly restless, too full in my own skin. The idea of knowing Seth's underwear preferences and dressing to accommodate them is...

Surprisingly hot.

I avoid him and get into bed.

Sure, Seth is surprisingly sexy. But he's still *Seth*. If I make a move, it'll send him running to the room of icy death. If he's listening to my opinion on men's undershirts, it's probably because I'm the only woman under thirty-five who's ever *given* him an opinion on men's undershirts.

Seth turns off the main light, so all that's left is the little one by my bed, and gets under the covers.

He's doing the thing again where he's practically on the edge of the bed.

"How about you scoot like six inches in?" I say. "You don't want to fall off again."

"No, thank you," he says, looking about as relaxed as a corpse after rigor mortis has set in.

Whatever. I roll my eyes and turn my back to him. I saved Seth from hypothermia. It's his own damn fault if he doesn't know how to sleep in a bed without injuring himself.

"I'll fix the room thing tomorrow," Seth promises abruptly. "And get pajamas."

"That's what they all say," I mutter, and turn out the light.

***

I wake up with warm sunlight dappling my body and the unshakeable sense everything's going to be all right. It's such an unfamiliar sensation for me, I'm convinced I'm still dreaming until I figure out why I'm feeling so irrationally optimistic.

I'm tucked firmly and safely under Seth's chin. His heat radiates through me like one of those heavy sacks stuffed with herbs you heat up in the microwave and put on your neck to relax. His steady, deep breathing calms me better than white noise apps ever do. It's like waking up under his jacket on the airplane, but a hundred times better.

I should roll away. Heavy, sleepy Seth might be my personal Xanax, but he'd be mortified to wake up and find us cuddling. I'm about to scoot away, when he pulls me closer and tucks his face into my neck, breathing deeply. The appreciative sound he makes, deep in his throat? It's a very, very masculine sound.

And the way he's pressed up against my ass? My eyes widen.

Let's say that's appreciative and masculine too. *Very* appreciative.

He's not my boss anymore.

For a second, in our quiet, sunlit room, it seems like the world stops. Because I've got two paths before me. Roll away, act like this never happened, and spend the next month pretending everything between me and Seth is almost normal. Or arch into him like I want to, until he's awake in more ways than one, and seduce him before breakfast. I would have thought it impossible—Seth's never been anything but professional—but when he's not thinking, his body responds to mine.

And when he's thinking, he stops wearing undershirts for me.

He's not my boss anymore.

My heart is beating fast as I twist in his arms to face Seth.

A sharp knock on the door jolts him awake and me back to reality. I skitter back to the edge of the bed, flailing. My feet get caught in the sheets as I try to jump out of bed. I fall hard on the floor.

"Breakfast, y'all. There's quiche Lorraine," Barbie calls.

This time it's Seth who pokes his head over the bed to look down at me. His shirt has come unbuttoned at the collar, his hair is mussed, and there's a tantalizing five-o'clock shadow making good use of his cheekbones. My hormones do a little swoon because biology is a bitch.

"Are you ok?" Seth asks, his normally cultured voice gruff with sleep.

"Peachy," I say, trying to look past his gorgeous face and focus on the ceiling. It's a very well-crafted ceiling.

His smile is lazy and reminds me of late nights at the gallery, or those rare mornings when I'd come in to find he'd slept in the office.

"Do I want to know, Miss Smith?" he asks, and I close my eyes because it's the only way to hide his beautiful, inconveniently virtuous face.

"No, Mr. Moreau," I say. "You really don't."

***

After breakfast I'm alone in our room, getting as cute as I can for the engagement photo shoot Amelie's scheduled for today—although Lord knows why I care since it's a fake engagement with a man I'm never going to see again—when my phone pings with an incoming email.

Seth's set up the money in an escrow account like he promised. My email pings with a second email.

It's from Seth. I click.

I've attached a letter giving you my unqualified recommendation for any position you should choose to take next. Normally I'd wait until you request a reference, so I could customize it for the specific position, but I realize this next month will undoubtedly introduce certain changes to our relationship, and I would like you to have every assurance possible your work as an administrative assistant is a separate matter I always have, and always will, respect you for.

I've attached three separate versions of the letter, one aimed at future employers, one aimed at educational and development programs you may wish to apply to, and one aimed at everything else.

I realize this may be impossible, but I should like you to feel equal in this (admittedly bizarre) endeavor of ours. Because you are.

Please let me know if you have issues opening any of the attachments. You're normally the one who tests stuff like that.

—S

I blink at my phone, realizing my eyes are watering.

How dare he. How fucking *dare* he.

I'd said I was quitting but somehow this… this makes it real.

That's definitely why I'm fighting tears. Because it's the end of a time when I felt like I had a safe port to rest.

It's not because one of the New York art world's most successful men wrote, without a trace of irony or false modesty, that he respects me unconditionally and considers me his equal.

There's a rap on the door.

"Hurry up, darling," Amelie calls. "The photographer's here."

"Coming." I hastily wipe my eyes and set my phone aside without bothering to confirm Seth's attachments open. Part of disappearing means not using your old employers for a reference.

But the fact he thought to write them? That matters.

That matters a lot.

Chapter Nine

Seth

Amelie's photographer, Jane, is a cheerful, freckled Black woman with bright blue hair who declares we'll be doing shots in two locations. Some on the steps in front of the chateau, and others in the back in front of the gardens.

Victor and I sit on the steps in our suits waiting for our respective fiancées to show up.

"I've got an idea," Jane says encouragingly. "Let's get some shots of you brothers together."

"No," Victor and I say in unison. Jane takes a step back under the force of our animosity.

The door squeaks and bangs as it's thrown open, and we both turn as Amelie, Barbie, and Darcy join us.

I do a double take when I see Darcy. Simply looking at her pulls me to my feet, like I'm in some sort of fairy tale, standing when the heroine walks into the room.

She's in a delicate ice blue dress which fits her like a glove before flaring out at the waist in yards of fluffy, almost sheer fabric ending above her knees. The fine silver jewelry she's got on completes the Cinderella look, but those deep red velvet ankle boots with sky-high heels are all Darcy. No glass slippers for my girl.

Barbie's wearing something pink with pockets. I know this because all the women are excited about the pockets.

"Ok," Jane calls. "First let's get a classic portrait of each couple in front of the chateau. Then we'll move on to some of the more fun, candid shots. We'll definitely be done within three hours."

Three hours? Darcy and I look at each other in alarm.

Even Barbie looks unnerved.

Amelie looks like the cat that ate the cream.

Jane positions Darcy and me on the steps and instructs everyone else to clear the shot.

It's a relatively painless experience. Hand hovering on Darcy's waist. Smile for the camera. Hand hovering on Darcy's shoulder. Smile for the camera. Step behind Darcy, hands hovering over her hips, smile for the camera. Wash, rinse, repeat.

Except it goes on. And on. And on.

"Ok, try facing each other, and looking deeply into each other's eyes," Jane calls, and we shuffle to follow her instructions. I hover my hands over Darcy's waist. She hovers her hands over my shoulders. I feel like we're at an awkward high school dance.

Victor snickers.

"Did you take this many photographs for your last wedding?" I ask Darcy under my breath.

"Lie back and think of England," she mutters behind the world's most brilliant smile. The camera flashes, and I choke back a laugh.

"No, don't hide the laugh. Have fun," Jane trills out.

Darcy raises an eyebrow. "I think I know how we can get this over with. Do you trust me?"

I shrug. "Sure."

She grabs the lapels of my jacket, rises on her toes, and kisses me.

My head explodes. She's so soft, and hot, and the way she smells... I inhale sharply, and she slides her tongue into my mouth.

Dear God. I'm drowning in Darcy. My hands tighten on her waist, reflexively, and she gives a little purr of encouragement, so soft I don't know if I hear it or feel it.

I don't remember pulling her close or sinking my hands into her hair, but apparently I do, because that's where I am when she pulls back.

The photographer is saying something, but I'm not listening. I'm staring at Darcy's mouth. The mouth that was kissing me a second ago. The one smiling at me now.

"Seth. You're blocking the shot," Darcy says.

"What?" I say dumbly. *You kissed me.*

Darcy takes my right hand and moves it from her hair to her waist so my arm isn't blocking her face from the camera.

Right. The camera. The reason we're doing this in the first place.

"Someone needs to get laaaaaid," Victor sings, *sotto voce*, because brothers.

"Ignore him," Darcy says. "Ignore everything but me."

"That could be dangerous," I mutter, looking at her lips.

Darcy's gray eyes widen. "Seth Moreau. Are you *flirting* with me?"

"Stating a fact."

"Oh my god. You *are* flirting with me."

I fight back a smile unsuccessfully, and the camera clicks.

It's almost painful, her smile. Because I'm not trying to flirt with her. I'm not. But her kiss is like the moon, pulling in a tide of every thought I ever ignored or pushed down. All the things I wasn't supposed to say before because she worked for me. All the things I'm not supposed to say now, because putting up with me wanting her was never supposed to be part of the half a million dollars.

"Kiss her again," Jane instructs. "But don't block her face this time."

"You got it," I say, and lower my lips to Darcy's.

Something flashes in Darcy's eyes, and there's enough alarm there for me to stop, a hair's breadth from her mouth.

There's the flash of more photos.

"Oooo, very romantic, y'all," Barbie calls. "Like those Nicholas Sparks covers."

Darcy looks up from my mouth, surprised. "What are you waiting for?"

"Do you trust me?" I ask, so quietly, only she can hear.

She bites her lip. The way she's searching my face while nerves flicker across hers hurts more than it should.

Of course she doesn't trust me. Not for this. *Power dynamics exist.*

I paste a smile on my face and turn away from her. "We're hogging the spotlight. Let Barbie and Victor have a go."

"But if you could just—" Jane tries, but I'm already leading Darcy down the steps while Barbie gamely takes the spotlight.

Five minutes of watching Victor and Barbie convinces me they're not a real couple. Instead of the hover-touch I was doing, Barbie grips his shoulder like it's the first step in a complicated self-defense move that will result in Victor tumbling down the stone steps.

"Why didn't you kiss me?" Darcy asks quietly. "She didn't get the shot."

"It's a fake shoot for a fake engagement. It doesn't matter if she gets the shot."

"We still have to convince Amelie—"

"You said you didn't trust me." The realization sits in my body like a fresh bruise.

On the steps, Jane tries to convince Victor to dip Barbie, and Barbie shakes her head like a bobblehead on speed.

Darcy looks up at me. "Seth. I didn't say—"

"You hesitated." She doesn't deny it, and that's how I know I'm making the right decision. "As long as you hesitate, I'm not kissing you. No matter how bossy everyone gets with this wedding crap. Next time someone tries to make us kiss, you kiss me. And if you don't, I'll know you aren't comfortable and get us out of the situation. Understand?"

This time when Darcy nods, there's no hesitation. Her face is a clear blue sky unmarred by doubts.

My whole body relaxes. "Good."

I turn back to the photo shoot in time to watch Barbie accidentally elbow Victor in the stomach.

***

It's the longest three hours of my life. After we finish in front of the chateau, we move to the gardens. Jane solves the problem of Barbie and Victor's general antagonism by having them chase each other, arm wrestle, and actually wrestle. By the time she's finished photoshopping, it will probably look cute and quirky instead of like the Hunger Games in a suit and heels.

Darcy, for her part, takes control of our shots. It's three drugging hours of her draping herself against me, caressing me, running her hands through my hair, kissing me.

Hell, the *kissing*. Darcy has a mouth on her, in more ways than one.

Now and then I'm called on to lift her in the air, or spin her in a circle, but other than that, it's the Darcy show.

Kissing her is heaven. Holding myself back is hell. Fighting off a hard-on is a feat of pure willpower and I want a goddamn trophy.

By the time Jane finally announces she's got what she needs, I'm wound so tight I can't think straight. I need a cold shower now. Maybe I should tell Darcy no more kissing during this whole engagement thing, for either of us.

The obvious flaw is then she'd stop kissing me.

I'm a strong man. In control of myself, of my desires. But it turns out I'm not strong enough to ask Darcy Smith to stop kissing me.

We're heading into the house for dinner, and I'm considering the mess I've gotten myself into when Darcy catches my hand. Her strong fingers thread through mine. She kisses me quickly, softly, on the cheek.

It's a chaste kiss, nothing at all compared to the performance she's been putting on for the last three hours.

But there's no camera. Everyone else is up ahead of us.

My heart fumbles.

"You're a good man, Seth. A really, really good man." Darcy squeezes my hand in easy friendship.

And like that, the last three hours are worth it.

Chapter Ten

Darcy

Seth's as good as his word (of course he is) and finds a room to sleep in upstairs not recently painted and open to the elements.

No word yet on if he's acquired pajamas.

I suppose he could borrow some from Victor. I picture straitlaced Seth in Victor's preferred silk or velvet, and I snort a laugh as I finish hanging up my dress and lining up my red boots by my suitcase.

I put my hands on my hips and look around the room. I can't shake the feeling something's missing.

My eyes fall on Seth's side of the bed.

No, that's not it. You do not get used to someone's weight at your back in two days.

Besides, since he's not here, I can stay up late reading my romance novel, which as far as I'm concerned is the point of a vacation.

Are you really living your best life if you're not sleep-deprived the next day from reading about the trials and tribulations of fictional people?

I turn out all the lights but my bedside lamp and burrow under the covers. I crack open my book with a sigh of almost sensual contentment.

That's where the trouble begins. Normally I can fall straight into a story, but the hero is inconveniently tall and dark-haired, and I keep finding myself accidentally picturing Seth. To the point when the hero passionately kisses the heroine into submission, I find myself wrinkling my nose and shaking my head. *Nope. Not how Seth kisses.*

No, Seth kisses like he's at the kind of restaurant it takes years to get a reservation at, and you're what's on the menu.

I slide restlessly in the sheets.

Do you trust me?

Yes and no, I would have said, if I was being honest. *Yes and no. In the most delicious, terrifying way.*

"Ugh." I shove the book aside, roll over onto my back, and stare up at the ceiling. I can't get his kisses out of my head. It's my punishment for using a fake engagement photo shoot to satisfy the curiosity I'd woken up with.

He shouldn't trust me. I've been lying to him about my past. About my name. And now, apparently, about how I want to jump his bones.

He's not your boss anymore.

I groan and roll over to turn the lights off. This is midnight talking. As soon as I wake up, I'll remember Seth's a dork. I'll remember how insane it makes me when he tries to add meetings to the office calendar himself and screws up my system. I'll remember the huge power disparity, no matter how many letters of recommendation he writes, and no matter how many times I tell him not to apologize.

I'll remember he doesn't know me at all.

***

After what feels like hours of restless tossing and turning, and smacking myself in the forehead every time I have an inappropriate thought about Seth, I give up and check the time on my phone.

It's been sixteen minutes.

"Fuck me," I say into the dark void of the bedroom.

Knowing what Seth kissed like when I caught him off guard... it feels like a taste of what he'd be like if this were real. If it weren't for cameras. Focused, and intense, and completely oblivious to everything around us.

And it's killing me.

Then there's the way he kept closing his eyes before I kissed him. If it weren't for the way I could feel his pulse racing under my fingertips, and the way his breath stuttered, I'd think he was unaffected.

Seth is very, very affected by me. But instead of taking advantage of the situation like I did, he closed his eyes and waited, for whatever I wanted to do to him. I never thought I'd be into a strong man putting himself at my mercy like that, but damn. When the man is Seth? How am I supposed to get it out of my head?

The answer is, I'm not. Right now, in the dark of night, alone in my bed, I am incapable of getting how Seth kisses, how he reacts to my touch, out of my head.

Oh, screw it. If there's no way off this particular self-destructive train, I might as well get some enjoyment out of it. Some goddamn relief.

Memory gives in to fantasy as I slide my hand low and picture Seth, waiting for my lips. Only this time we're somewhere private and there's no reason for me not to bury my hands in his hair, wrap my legs around his waist, stroke him where he's helplessly hard (of course he's hard, it's my fantasy), rip his expensive shirt off...

The great thing about fantasies is I don't have to worry about things like flexibility, stamina, or physics.

Or the fact Seth would probably get all prim and proper if I tried to do half the things I'm picturing, saying *Miss Smith* in the strained tone he uses whenever I needle him too much.

That strained voice is taking on new meaning, now I know how physically responsive he is to me. Except this time, in my head? He's saying my real name.

Miss Sherwood.

I moan, working myself with the hand wearing his ring. That rich, rolling pleasure is climbing, and I'm almost there, *Oh Seth, yes, there, YES—*

The door slams open, and I yank my hand away as the lights flick on.

"There are *bats* in my *room*," Seth screeches, his eyes wild behind his spectacles, a man who has been pushed too far to the edge. "*Bats*, Darcy."

I could push him to the edge.

I yank my mind out of the fantasy and into the present.

Which is I'm incredibly horny, but I can't come, because the object of my fantasies has arrived because there are bats in his room.

"Think of them as organic bug control," I say helpfully.

"No. No, I draw the line. They *fly*, Darcy. Over your head. Just...*VROOM*. Flying mouse. There it goes." He checks to make sure the door behind him is locked, like maybe the bats will develop a sudden proficiency with doorknobs. He hits the light switch and crawls into bed, muttering darkly about final straws and the collapse of civilization.

I can't believe it. I practically had to give a TED talk to convince him to sleep in the same bed as me before. And now tonight is when he decides to take me at my word? A few seconds later and I could have...

"You know, it's kind of wimpy, to be this scared of nature," I say. "Maybe you should go back and face your fears. So you can grow. As a man."

"That's enough, Miss Smith," he says in his stern, sexy, British voice of his which means he's not going anywhere.

The voice that is currently tying my fantasy and reality into one tangled, unsatisfying knot.

***

At least there's cheese, I reflect twelve hours later, as a waiter sets a plate of charcuterie before me. Amelie split everyone up today, which means Seth and I are enjoying a peaceful tasting at the restaurant that will be doing the catering for our double wedding, while Barbie and Victor will get drunk sampling the wine options somewhere. Amelie is either meeting her girlfriend or painting in peace. It's a toss-up.

We're at a small table by the window where we can watch the world go by, as much as the world goes in a sleepy, medieval stone town. The walls and cobblestones and old buildings would feel too gray, but the sun is warm, and there are little touches of light, plants, and color everywhere I look. Vines growing up and over stone walls. A woman in a yellow dress. The jewel-blue sky makes me think of Seth's eyes.

I stamp on the thought. It's one thing to lust after an objectively attractive man whose breath hitches when you kiss him. It's another thing entirely to go all moony over his eyes.

I point to the yellow flower sitting in a small blue vase on our table. "What's this? It smells like honeysuckle."

"Yellow broom flowers," Seth answers absently, spreading soft cheese on a cracker. "I don't know why Amelie's going through the motions of a tasting. We could be seeing Monet's gardens for you, or—"

"We've got a whole month to see Monet's gardens. Look on the bright side."

Seth arcs an eyebrow. "The bright side?"

"No Victor. No Barbie. Amazing food. An adorable French street with three art galleries. And no Amelie, so no need to pretend."

The chef emerges to check how we're doing, and Seth casually catches my hand, kissing the inside of my wrist. The restaurant isn't officially open right now—they're doing the tasting as a special favor to Amelie—and my heart thumps in the gentle silence of the empty room.

I pull my hand away as the chef unceremoniously sets an open bottle of white wine and two glasses on the table.

"Oh, we're not—"

The chef says something in French, looks at Seth, and goes back to the kitchen. I look at Seth questioningly.

"He says without wine, we can't know what it will truly taste like," Seth says, trying not to laugh. "I think we're in trouble for not getting our wine here too."

"Oh good. Just what I need. Someone with a large collection of professionally sharpened knives mad at me."

Seth smiles, free and joyful, and my heart catches. I thought I was romanticizing how great his smile was the day I met him, but there it is, right there across the table from me. For two years, he's been hiding that smile. Or at least not bringing it to the office.

Seth pours the wine. He casually swirls his before sipping, like people who have been drinking expensive wine since they were sixteen do.

I gulp mine. It's easy for him to be casual. He's not sitting across from that smile.

Seth settles back in his chair with his glass, nodding to my wrist. "Sorry about that. I think we still have to pretend a little."

"What? Oh no. It's fine. I, uh, didn't realize you were doing kissing now. Yesterday you said it was up to me when we… you caught me off guard…"

Seth looks stricken. "I didn't even think… Wrists count?"

When you do it like that, they do.

Maybe that's why I splutter, "No, no, they don't have to. Why would they?"

"Ok," he says.

"Ok," I say.

We stare at each other over wine and cheese in a foreign country, at a loss for words.

"Here," Seth says abruptly, spreading cheese on bread and passing it to me. "It's a tasting menu. We should taste."

"That would be a reasonable action, given the relationship dynamics we're trying to portray," I say, mimicking his robot voice from two weeks ago in the office.

Seth points the cheese knife at me. "Brat."

I smile, but I'm thinking of the office I'm never going to see again. The gallery shows I won't be a part of. I can't help but feel a sense of loss.

A lot of it has to do with the man across the table from me. A man who is more scared of bats than hypothermia. Who scoffs at spending a few hundred on first-class airfare but will drop half a million to preserve the legacy of someone he loves. Who won't let himself kiss me, but whose heart races when I kiss him.

A man I can't ever see again. It has to be a clean break if I ever want to be free of Victor, and safe from my past mistakes.

Seth looks out the window, thinking. I'm hit with a sudden desire to know him as well as I can before I go. I don't want to leave still wondering who the man quietly working on the other side of the office wall really was.

I open my mouth to ask something, anything, but it's surprisingly terrifying. What if Seth's irritated, and we spend the last month in huffy silence? What if he answers in a way that knocks him off the pedestal I've built for him?

Seth sips his wine, the epitome of Instagram-boyfriend-porn.

Just do it. Something easy. Not personal. "So when did you know you were attracted to me?" I blurt, and he chokes on his wine.

"What?" he says, whipping his attention to me. "If I've made you uncomfortable at all—"

"You haven't made me uncomfortable. We're young, we get along. It's a normal physical reaction."

"*Miss Smith.*"

"Don't *Miss Smith* me. I don't work for you. And after yesterday's… *successful* photo shoot, I'm curious. How long have you known you were attracted to me? Was it when we took the pictures on your phone to show Amelie?"

I realize I'm gesturing with the cheese and bread he handed me, like a madwoman, so I stuff it in my mouth.

I blink. *Oh God. That's good.*

I grab the cheese knife from him and start piling cheese onto a piece of bread. It's not the tasteful amount Seth did. No, this sucker is an ode to salt and cream and utter deliciousness. I take a bite.

"What's your real name?" Seth asks, and I choke on the bread.

I wash it down with wine, something which would no doubt horrify the chef. "Why does it matter?"

"Why does my being attracted to you matter?" He pushes his glasses up his nose and tries to look at me sternly, but it's undercut by the blush on his cheeks.

I narrow my eyes, but Seth doesn't flinch. He blushes a little harder.

What the hell. Victor already knows my real name and I'll be gone in a month.

"Fine," I say, toasting him with my wineglass. "I'll tell you my last name. If you tell me how long you've known you were attracted to me."

He straightens, like he's surprised I agreed, but nods eagerly.

I look down at the amber of my wineglass. This is what I've wanted since Victor stole my name from me, but it's harder than I expected.

I take another swig of wine for courage, then meet Seth's eyes. "Sherwood," I say. "Darcy Sherwood."

"Darcy Sherwood," he repeats.

"Yup. So about that inconvenient attraction of yours—"

"Miss Sherwood," he says like he's trying it out, and *hello*. It is flat-out rude of the man to be acting out my fantasies in public.

I take a slice of pear, enjoying the soft, cool sweetness against my tongue. "Your turn," I say brightly, reaching for more cheese.

"Since the sidewalk," he says, and my mouth goes dry.

He can't mean... there must have been a moment on the sidewalk more recently than...when we met.

But I'm coming up blank.

"You mean..."

"When you ran into me, that first day," Seth says helpfully. "You were wearing a dark sweater, and these black boots, like you were so tough. But you had this necklace that was kind of...floaty. Silvery. It made me think of..." He trails off. "You don't remember any of this. Never mind."

He remembers what I was wearing the first day we met?

Seth clears his throat. "It's not like I've been...you know. Thinking about it... Once I got to know you..."

"Hey, rude."

"That's not what I meant I... You don't think about your employee like that. So I didn't."

I put the cheese down. "Just like that."

Seth looks down, his hands restless on the table. "I mean, there may have been the occasional moment. Here and there. But you don't give in to them."

I flash guiltily to last night. Clearly Seth is made of sterner stuff because I very much *gave in*, as he would put it.

He takes the knife from me, precisely slicing a bit of cheese which he lays on bread, before carefully placing a slice of pear on top.

"But yes," Seth says. I'm so fixated by the elegance of his hands and the precision of his movements, I've forgotten what question he's answering. "Taking the photos in my office was one of those moments, despite my best efforts."

He looks up at me from under lowered lashes. "Do you hate me, Miss Sherwood?"

I hesitate. Because this would be so much easier if I hated him. If this felt like a breach of faith. And Lord knows, there have been enough people I've worked for—Victor springs to mind—where a confession like this would make me squirm with discomfort at best, or dangerous with righteous fury at worst.

But Seth would have gone to the grave never telling me if I hadn't argued it out of him.

Delicious anticipation flirts and sparks under my skin. Did I argue it out of him because some part of me wanted *Always* to be his answer?

The chef appears, replacing the charcuterie board with a series of desserts. This time he speaks in heavily accented English for my benefit. "Mademoiselle Moreau does not want a full meal for the wedding. She requested, 'only the good stuff.' I have many suitable meals if she should change her mind."

I look from the crème brûlée to the chocolate mousse to the apple tart thing. "Are we picking between the three?"

"*Non.* All three are 'the good stuff.'" He vanishes into the kitchen before I can tell him I'm not done with the cheese.

I evaluate my options judiciously because I do love chocolate, but well, how often do you eat crème brûlée in France?

I lift a spoon to crack the sugar crust.

"Oh for God's sake," Seth bursts out. "Tell me."

I blink.

"Tell you...?"

"If you hate me," he bites out. "Or..."

"Or?"

"You kissed me. Was it just acting?" Seth's gaze is so intense, it's a physical thing. He wants me, but he also wants the truth of me. I have the eerie feeling if I give it to him, everything between us will spiral out of my control.

I look down at the crème brûlée. I dip my spoon into the silky vanilla crème, trying to give myself time to think. This getting to know people isn't for suckers. It didn't occur to me he might want to know me back.

"Right." Seth puts his elbow on the table, his face in his hand. "Of course it was acting. I'm sorry I said anything. I shouldn't have... Of course, you don't—"

I reach out to touch his arm, my engagement ring glinting in the sunlight, and he looks up. "I don't hate you. And it wasn't acting. It was..." I wave the spoon with my other hand, searching for something that will be true, but also safe. "Vacation."

Seth frowns. "Vacation?"

"Haven't you ever pretended you were something else, even for a little while?"

"I'm pretending to be your fiancé."

"No, for fun."

He studies me, then grabs a spoon and, pulling the chocolate mousse closer to him, digs in. He doesn't say anything, and I don't know if it's because the chocolate is that good, or because he's thinking it over.

"So," he says without looking up, "you're saying what we're doing is fun, but not real?"

I nod, relieved he understands. "Yes. Exactly. You're ok with that, right?"

He dips his spoon into the chocolate, then holds it across the table to me. "Here. Try this."

I frown because sharing food is very un-Seth-like behavior. He nods subtly toward the kitchen, where the chef is lingering in the doorway. Probably waiting to see if we like his lovingly crafted desserts.

So I open my mouth and let Seth feed me the most delicious chocolate I've ever had in my life. It's dark and bitter and creamy, and the crème brûlée was good, but this…

This is decadent. It's like discovering kinky sex after a lifetime of polite missionary. I lick the corner of my mouth to get the last bit.

"More," I say, and when Seth obliges, his eyes are dark. So dark I almost don't taste the chocolate. I swallow, feeling like I can't look away. Vacations can get out of control too.

His eyes drop to my mouth, and I resist the urge to squirm in my seat.

"Fun but not real." Seth raises his eyes to mine. And for some reason, his smile feels forced. "Why wouldn't I be fine with that? It's every man's dream, right?"

"Right," I say.

But I avoid the chocolate and go back to the crème brûlée. It's a much safer choice. And I've used up all my bravery for one afternoon.

Chapter Eleven

Seth

Darcy dashes from shop window to shop window, delighted by everyone and everything. She's a whirl of motion, her ridiculous purple coat flaring with every step she takes.

As I follow behind, it dawns on me I don't know why the hell I'm doing any of this anymore. Amelie doesn't care about what Victor will do to her legacy. All she cares about is which of us is most likely to have a kid, which is pretty rich coming from someone who has been happily childless her entire life. The money I'm spending to get Darcy to lie is going to screw me over financially for years to come. I've officially lost the best administrative assistant I ever had. And now, to top it all off, Darcy says we're fun but not real.

I don't know why that digs at me. We're *not* real—we're faking a damn engagement.

Darcy disappears gleefully into what is either a completely disorganized art gallery, or a very well-decorated art supply store. I sit down on the wrought-iron bench outside and cross my arms, staring glumly ahead.

An elderly couple strolls by hand in hand, him in a cap, her in a red hijab. She's waving her free hand to illustrate her point as she speaks rapid-fire French. He doesn't say anything but smiles in a deep, contented way of a man long in love.

I glance back through the store window. Darcy's speaking quickly and energetically, her hands flying through the air in an attempt to cross the cultural barrier and communicate what she needs.

It's probably pride, I think. If I'm going to tell someone I've been attracted to her for years, it would be nice if her reaction wasn't "eh, not real." Because it feels more real than any of the dates I've been on since I met her.

Maybe Darcy's right. Maybe I've been stuffing my emotions down for so long, I've completely lost touch with something as simple as what attraction is supposed to feel like.

A bell rings as the shop door opens, and Darcy leans out. "Seth, I need you. She's trying to tell me the story of this painting and I don't understand it."

"Good. That keeps you from being distracted by a sales pitch and will help you judge the painting on its own merits," I say, but Darcy rolls her eyes.

"It's not for sale. It's a family treasure. I understood that much. Now come on."

She heads into the store, completely convinced I'll follow wherever she goes.

So I do.

As soon as I'm in the shop, I'm hit with a wave of memory. I've been here before, as a kid. Amelie would come to pick up art supplies, and I would wander through the paintings. Actual impressionist paintings from the 1800s are sprinkled in among more modern paintings, done in the same style. It's all color and blur. Light and loose brushstrokes. I remember taking off my glasses as a kid and squinting, trying to make the world look like it did in all these paintings.

Darcy's in the back with the shopkeeper, who looks familiar— broad, auburn-haired, sharp eyes, gentle voice.

They're both standing in front of a painting that takes my breath away. I don't know why—it's a simple pastoral scene, a woman in white running happily past hedges on a sunny day. There's nothing daring, shocking, or original about it at all. But looking at it, it's like I can feel the warmth of the sun on my skin, feel the woman's happiness. If I looked at its components, I'd find nothing extraordinary about this painting, but despite years of training, I am physically incapable of looking at it as anything but a whole.

"What did she say, Seth?"

I snap my attention to Darcy. "What?"

The shopkeeper repeats herself, gesturing to the paintings. It takes me a moment. She's got the accent of someone whose family has been in the area for generations. But eventually, my brain clicks into her phrasing, and I figure it out.

"She's saying this painting was made by a local artist, Vivian LaBlanc, in the 1800s. But no one knew that until years after her death. During her lifetime, all Vivian's paintings were attributed to her male teacher."

"But...why?"

"Sexism?" I guess.

Darcy hits me in the arm. "No. Ask her. I want the real answer."

So I do. The shopkeeper's face goes sad even before she starts answering, something Darcy picks up on immediately.

I translate. "Vivian was from a good family, but not so good they could afford an eccentric daughter. Some skill at painting was acceptable for young women, but Vivian wanted to paint more than beautiful flowers and sweet portraits. So she made a deal with her parents and teacher. She would be allowed to paint what she wanted, so long as it was attributed to the teacher. He would then sell it, and her parents would receive a portion of the profits."

The shopkeeper rummages through a rack of more tourist-friendly items and returns with a small, printed book of paintings by Vivian. She flips through the book, pointing out paintings that would have seemed scandalous for an unmarried woman at the time. Dancers in clubs, men at salons, couples racing through the rain together. It's all cool tones shot through with light, with movement, with people reaching for each other.

The shopkeeper passes the book to Darcy, her voice gentle. Then she looks at me expectantly.

"She says it was not so bad," I translate. "She painted what she wanted, until she died in a carriage accident in Paris in her early thirties. It was a kind of freedom."

"*No*," Darcy says, so viciously I'm startled. "That is *not* freedom."

Darcy points to a corner on the painting where a name has been precisely scratched into the corner. *Maurice Robinson*. It's the only careful thing on the whole painting.

"If she had to put someone else's name to it," Darcy says, her voice cracking, "she wasn't free."

I put my hand on her back, rubbing gentle circles. "Hey. It's ok." I don't know what's bothering Darcy, but something is.

She shrugs off my touch.

"*Merci,*" Darcy says to the shopkeeper and turns to go.

"Darcy, wait. Don't you want something...?" She's already out the door.

I hastily thank the shopkeeper and jog after Darcy, catching up to her easily on the cobblestone streets.

"What was that about?" I ask.

"I don't want to talk about it." Her jaw is tight, her movements staccato.

"If you're not in the mood to shop anymore, we can go back—"

"No," Darcy says.

So we walk in silence, taking turn after turn until even I'm a little lost. Still, Darcy doesn't look at me.

"Look, if you want to be alone—"

"You don't know everything about me," Darcy bursts out.

"I realize that," I say, but she's shaking her head, like there's no way I could ever understand. Something in the stubborn set of her jaw and the distance of her eyes reminds me of when she told me she was already married.

"Is this something to do with your past? The reason you changed your name?" The people you're trying to protect yourself from?

Darcy doesn't say anything.

"Were you not... did you not feel free?" I ask gently, and she stops, whirling to face me.

"You can't understand. It's like you're asking if I felt like I couldn't see or hear. You have been so free your whole life you can't even imagine..." She bites her nails like she's biting off the urge to say more. I want to tell her to spit it out. I want to know who trapped her, so I can hunt them down. I want to know why she felt trapped, so I can make sure she never is again.

But forcing someone to talk about something painful is its own kind of trap. Besides, it's none of my business. We're not real.

"I'm sorry," I say.

Darcy shrugs and looks away. "It's fine. How could you understand?"

"That's not what I was apologizing for." Something in my voice must register my seriousness because when she looks up at me, it's like she's really seeing me.

God, those eyes. A man could lose his bearing in Darcy's storm-gray eyes.

"I'm sorry whatever happened to you happened," I say. "You didn't deserve it."

Her shoulders and chin jerk. "Shows how much you know. It was my fault. My decision. I'm not some damsel in distress who's suddenly surprised when there are consequences for sneaking into the ball."

"I know you deserve to be free," I say simply. She wraps her arms around herself and looks away, as if what I'm saying is physically painful, and what we're talking about isn't in the past at all.

"Darcy," I say, "are you in trouble? Still? Because it's easy enough to track down a marriage license if they think to look. If whoever this is can hurt you…"

"It's fine, Seth."

"If it wasn't, would you let me help?"

She searches my face. "Why would you care? I'm not your fiancée. I'm not your employee."

"You're my friend," I say, and she blinks in surprise.

"Unless…that's not real, either." The loss hits me like the moment you realize a good dream isn't real. For months after Victor betrayed me, I'd wake up from dreams we weren't fighting, that I'd been confused. That he was my brother again. But every time I showed up at the office in a foul mood, there was Darcy to tease me out of it.

I thought we were friends, but maybe she's been humoring the boss. *God, I'm an idiot.* I never misread signals like this. But with Darcy, I'm a bull in a china shop.

"Sorry," I say, more abruptly than I mean to. I try for a joke. "I'm still getting the hang of this vacation thing."

I turn away and start walking, but I'm stopped by a small hand sliding into mine. Touching her feels like an anchor in a storm, though I'm not sure if the storm is mine or hers. I look down at Darcy, who stares straight ahead as if she didn't just take my hand.

"We're as real as we can be," she says. "I don't think it would be real, at all, with anyone else."

Something in my heart eases. I squeeze her hand. "Are you ready to go home now?"

Darcy looks around the peaceful old street like she's memorizing it. Then she nods.

"Yeah. We can go home."

***

She's pensive on the way home, like she can't shake the weight of whatever's worrying her. And I find I can't shake the weight of an unhappy Darcy.

What makes Darcy happy?

Painting. I think of how at peace she was when she was painting with Amelie.

When we pass the art store that started all of this, I reluctantly pull my hand from hers. "One moment."

"Seth—"

"Give me a minute."

I go inside, truly intending to only be a minute, but the shopkeeper is delighted I'm back, even more delighted to find out I'm buying paints for "the pretty girl with the big heart." By the time she's got me set up with her finest paints and brushes and a paint sketchbook (canvases won't travel well on a plane), it's been almost ten minutes. She's ringing me up when I throw in the Vivian LaBlanc book on impulse.

When I emerge from the store, Darcy's got her own shopping bag.

I look down at it with an arched brow.

"You've got your secrets." She smiles. "I've got mine."

It's such a relief to see her smiling again so I take her hand and start swinging it as we walk along. Darcy laughs, but she doesn't pull away.

"So," I say. "I hear Amelie wants to take you and Barbie wedding dress shopping in Paris. Do you want me to get you out of it?"

"Don't you dare. One of the places she wants to take us to is so famous it's basically like a museum. Of course, it's utterly ridiculous they'd have anything ready to go in a month—think of the tailoring, and that's not even getting into the cost..." Darcy's chattering happily away, using her free hand to illustrate the wonderful absurdity of it all. I smile, happy to listen.

It's not my first choice, but if this is what I have... maybe I can get into this whole vacation thing. It's not like you can fall for a girl just from listening to her talk.

Chapter Twelve

Darcy

I fold the pajamas I bought and carefully place them on Seth's side of the bed. At this point the pretense he'll be sleeping anywhere else is ridiculous. Which is why I got him some very nice, very dignified pajamas.

It is a truth universally acknowledged men don't look sexy in real pajamas. I've known plenty of men who can pull off low-slung sweats and a soft, dark, fitted t-shirt. I have known men who can pull off boxers.

I have yet to meet a man who can pull off old-school, *Leave it to Beaver* button-up pajamas. I almost picked light blue to match Seth's eyes, but I ended up going with a stately dark gray with navy piping.

I grin down at the pajamas. There's a good chance Seth hates them. I can also kind of imagine him liking them. Wouldn't it be ironic if he likes them and keeps wearing them after I'm gone?

There's a knock at the door, and Seth comes in. "Sorry it's late, I was scouting out rooms. I think I'm going to sleep on one of the living room couches and set an early alarm..." He trails off when he sees the pajamas.

"What are those?"

"You said you needed pajamas." I head around to my side of the bed.

"You didn't have to..." He reaches out a hand to feel the fabric, then looks up, alarmed. "These are nice. I can pay you back—"

I roll my eyes. "I'm coming into some money. Take the gift, Moreau."

I throw back my covers, and there's a thump as a book falls to the floor.

A heavy book. An art book.

I bend to pick it up. I hadn't noticed it on the covers in the dim light, but it was definitely on my side of the bed.

Except Seth didn't get me a gag gift. When I pick it up, it's the Vivian LaBlanc book from the store.

"I, uh, got you paint supplies too." Seth pushes up his glasses. "This part was…unplanned."

I flip through the book to be polite, torn. I do love the paintings. Vivian LaBlanc might be my new favorite painter. I'm touched Seth got me anything. He doesn't even participate in the office Secret Santa. He thinks if you're going to thrust a poorly chosen gift on someone, you should at least have the gumption to sign your name to it.

The book is beautifully weighted in my hands, but I know the signature in the corner is there, on every single page. And I know it's a different situation—Vivian wasn't committing a crime, for starters—but it's hitting way too close to home.

Robinson isn't Robin, but it feels like a warning all the same.

I look up in time to see Seth's face fall.

"You don't like what I did."

"No! No, I—"

"I can get you another one. One I didn't write in."

He wrote something? I flip toward the front, wondering if he wrote some sort of dedication (*To my favorite fake fiancée*, that sort of thing), and that's when I spot it.

On every painting, he's crossed out "Maurice Robinson" and written "Vivian LaBlanc."

My throat tightens. I stare down at the book in my hands. *God, this man.*

This is what he does for a woman he's not actually dating. Imagine what he'd do for someone he'd chosen… *I can't think like that.*

I make myself look up brightly and smile. "Thank you, Seth. You made it perfect."

He ducks his head, shy. "Thanks for the pajamas. I'll change, then head out to the couch."

"Oh, give it up." I throw a pillow at his head, and he ducks in surprise. "We both know you're going to end up back here. So let's skip the dance where you wake me up in the middle of the night. Ok?"

He hesitates. I throw another pillow at him.

He ducks and throws up his hands, not quite laughing, but I know where to look for the smile hidden in the corner of his mouth. "Ok, I surrender."

I smile. He goes into the bathroom to change, and I set my Vivian LaBlanc book on my bedside table reverently.

It takes me a moment to identify the emotion I feel, as I'm curled up under mounds of covers with a bible of gorgeous, inspiring art on my bedside table, and Seth about to turn in for the night too.

It's contentment.

***

It will come as no surprise to anybody Seth Moreau rocks old man pajamas. Very Gregory Peck.

My contentment goes up in smoke.

Fuck. My. Life.

***

Thirteen hours later I'm panting in Seth's arms.

Tragically, not the way I want to be. It's a dance class in Amelie's ballroom. Because of course she has a ballroom. The instructor is a slight, red-haired man in his forties. His sweater has holes in it, and his sense of grace is eerie.

Why are Seth, Victor, Barbie, and I taking dance classes for a double wedding that doesn't have a guest list and barely has a reception? No clue. It's like Amelie picked only the parts of wedding planning that give the couples an excuse to spend time with each other, or an excuse to touch each other. She's throwing everything else overboard like we're a sinking ship and she has to give us as little as possible to carry.

I would ask Amelie about it in one of our morning painting sessions, but I have no desire for her to add premarital counseling or picking stationery to the weirdest vacation of my life.

Seth twirls me around the ballroom, and it's delicious how well I flow in his arms. Seth is good at this. Who would have thought sits-behind-a-desk-all-day Seth had a sense of rhythm?

He turns us before we hit the wall, and now we're not traveling anymore. We're doing a sort of stylized swaying the dance instructor told the men to do whenever they needed a moment to steady themselves. We're dancing to some retro French jazz of Amelie's. As Seth guides me exactly where he wants me, his big hand spread on the small of my back, the old George Bernard Shaw line about dancing being a vertical expression of a horizontal desire floats through my head.

Seth spins me out, and I forget to hold my movements carefully, like the dance teacher taught us. Instead, I lean into the momentum, picking up speed, so when I get to the end of the spin, it's only the strength of Seth's arm stopping me from flying across the room. And when he tugs me back in, instead of stopping politely in front of him like I should, I crash into his chest, my hand splayed across his heart.

Which is how I can tell it's pounding.

And Seth? Seth's not panting. Whereas I am regretting my complete and total lack of an exercise regime, Seth is reaping the benefits of those holes in his calendar I leave—left—for running.

So if his heart is pounding? It's not because he's out of breath.

I look up, which is a mistake. His eyes are dark, and he's looking down at my mouth.

A horizontal desire indeed.

There's a crash and swearing, and I jerk my eyes away to see Barbie flinging Victor into the wall.

"What the hell?" Victor asks, rubbing his head.

"I was doing what he told me," Barbie drawls. "Wherever could I have gone wrong?" She turns and bats her eyes at the instructor. "Show me again?"

The instructor clears his throat. "Er…new plan. We're swapping partners."

"Hell no," Seth says, and his grip tightens. I don't know if he doesn't want me dancing with Victor, or if he fears what Barbie will do to him.

The instructor is insistent, and before I know it, Seth's on the other side of the room with Barbie, and Victor is smirking in front of me.

"Shall we?" He holds out a hand theatrically, but it still feels dangerous.

Reluctantly, I place one hand in his, the other on his shoulder. The instructor claps out the timing, and we start dancing.

It should feel similar, switching to a different brother. Victor and Seth are the same build, and they move with the same confident musicality. But where Seth is a generous partner—adding in more twirls because I like them, carefully guiding me through moves I struggle with, taking my lead on how close or far away I want to stand from him—Victor is selfish. His moves are unforgiving and precise. He expects you to do exactly what he wants, and if not, you end up bashing knees with him or having your arm yanked halfway out of its socket. The velvet of his jacket feels cloying after Seth's crisp cotton.

I try to ease back, in sudden sympathy with Barbie, but he pulls me in tighter.

I glance over to Barbie and Seth, but they're across the room, absorbed in what the instructor is saying.

Victor speaks into my ear, and the sourness of his breath makes my skin crawl. "I have a business proposition for you, Robin."

I stop dancing, but Victor won't allow it and forces us to sway.

"No," I grit out. "I'm done with that."

"You're not done until I say you are. I need an edge with my aunt. So you're going to paint me a Vivian LaBlanc. A never-before-seen one I will discover buried in a local shop."

He moves us farther away from the others. "She's Amelie's favorite painter. And I hear you have an affinity."

"I said no."

His claw of a hand on my back forces me closer. "I assumed I misheard you. Because you know if you don't do this for me, I'll expose you."

My heart is racing. I'm an animal, and I need to flee a predator. It's like the intervening years never happened. I'm a college dropout, trying to quit, and he's blackmailing me to stay like he did so many times before.

But it's not two years ago. I've grown stronger, braver, smarter.

Even better, I know his identity.

I push back against his hands, fighting for my own space. "If you turn me in to the police, I'll turn you in too."

"I'm not talking about the police," Victor says. "I'm talking about turning you in to Seth. He already hates me. But he likes you. I can end that. All I have to do is tell him the truth."

My stomach twists in instinctual fear at the thought of losing Seth.

"Fine," I bluff. "But I'll out you to Amelie if you say anything to Seth before the weddings. Then you'll never get this house."

He jolts me into a vicious spin.

"Why won't you do as you're told?"

Because you're threatening me with something I've already lost. I want Seth to think well of me when I'm gone. But if he doesn't? I'll be gone.

I force myself to laugh. "I guess I don't value yours or your brother's opinion as much as you think I do."

"You're proud. I'll give you that. But you won't be so proud when you've lost your job and your lover."

I shake my head, but Victor yanks me in and hisses. "I'm a generous man. So I'm going to give you time to think it over. Come up with whatever rationale you need to let yourself sleep at night. But if there's not a painting in my hands before the end of the month, Seth finds out who you really are as soon as the plane touches down."

I look him squarely in the eye. "I can live with that."

And then I take a page out of Barbie's book and stamp down squarely on his foot, angling my heel so it bites into his flesh with crippling pain.

"Bloody bitch," Victor swears, letting go of me.

Seth's at my side instantly. "What did you call her?"

"Ok. That's enough dancing for today." The instructor claps his hands. "We'll take this up tomorrow."

"No," I say, making sure Victor's looking at me. "We won't. We're through."

Seth puts a protective arm around me and escorts me out of the room.

It's not until Seth has us back in our bedroom, with the door locked behind us, I realize I'm shaking.

Seth tries to wrap me safely in his arms, but the memory of being trapped in Victor's is too fresh, and I flinch.

Seth steps back immediately. "I'm going to kill him."

"You don't even know what he said."

"I'm going to kill him."

I sink down onto a chaise and wrap my arms around myself. "No. Give... give me a moment."

I mean *Wait here with me*, but Seth misunderstands, turns on his heel, and leaves.

Or maybe he didn't misunderstand. Maybe he's tired of my mixed signals. One day I'm seducing him in front of a camera. The next day I'm telling him we're not real. Now I'm flinching when he touches me.

I put my head on my knees and breathe, trying not to think of how much he'll hate me when Victor tells him the truth.

I won't even be around to defend myself. Explaining it won't help. Seth doesn't have a gray area when it comes to crime.

For a moment I let myself fantasize about pretending to go along with Victor's scheme long enough to expose him for the fraud he is. But it's too dangerous. Anything I do would shine the same spotlight on me. Why risk it? Even if I *could* take down Victor, I don't exactly see Seth and I meeting up for collegial drinks.

My eyes sting with tears I flat-out refuse to cry. I hate Victor. I *hate* him. For the phone call, after he saw one of my paintings at an art show, asking if I did commissions. For the way he laughed when I showed up at his glitzy steel-and-chrome hotel room, bright-eyed with my portfolio. Most of all, I hate him for the money he offered. The money that seemed so big at the time, and so small in hindsight. The money that taught me I have a price.

I let out a strained laugh, seeing the events of the last few weeks in a new light. I was so proud of myself for spending the last few years building a new, honest life, but all I've done is raise the price. One engagement ring for a lie on FaceTime. A vacation in France for a lie in person. Half a million for a fake wedding.

I'm the exact same person I was. Worse, I'm dragging Seth down with me. Because now he knows he has a price too. A house and a legacy, for a lie to a loved one.

The door opens, and I snap my head up, worried it's Victor, but it's Seth.

He shuts the door behind him gently. Then he crosses to me, moving slowly like he doesn't want to scare me.

He kneels before me. "I talked to Amelie. We're going to Monet's house tomorrow."

"What?" I blink, confused by this sudden good thing amid a lonely, horrible day.

He keeps his voice low and soothing. "We're taking two days off from wedding stuff. If you want me to go with you, I will. If not, I'll get you to the gardens, then go catch up with work at the Paris gallery—"

I fling my arms around him, and he catches me, surprised.

"You didn't have to," I say into his neck.

"I promised," he says like it's the end of the conversation. And for Seth, it is.

I should pull back, but I can't. When I'm clutching his heat and strength, I feel strong enough to refuse Victor. Strong enough to let Seth go at the end of the month. I breathe in his scent and hold on.

Seth doesn't say anything, and he doesn't let go. He holds me as long as I need him.

***

The morning of our trip to Monet's garden, I wake up holding Seth's hand. We're far apart in the giant bed, but sometime in the night, our hands found each other.

I stare at him in the morning light, wishing I'd never come on this vacation. If I hadn't found out V. was Victor, and Victor hadn't found out his long-lost forger was hiding on his brother's payroll, I could have had years more of knowing Seth. Years of working side by side, of changing the lives of undiscovered artists, of teasing each other about coffee.

But then I never would have found out how essential his hand feels in mine, when his breathing is deep and even and the sun falls warm across his face, his black lashes beautifully stark against his cheek.

I squeeze his hand once, then let go.

I would have liked more years with this man.

***

With every mile we drive away from Amelie's, I relax.

Conversely, with each mile, Seth gets more tense. I fiddle with the radio and come across an oldies station playing French jazz which makes me think of Amelie.

"Not that," Seth says, and I look at him inquiringly.

"You were dancing with *him* to it," he says, his knuckles tight on the wheel, and I realize that's why the song is familiar. It was one of the ones we were dancing to yesterday.

I flip obligingly to a channel playing fast, furious French rap. To my surprise, Seth's face lights up.

"You know this song?" I ask.

"I love this song. They played it all summer long when I was seventeen." He starts rapping along, at first under his breath, stumbling a bit, then growing more confident as his tongue remembers the foreign words.

I have no idea what he's saying, but he's saying it with passion and energy and a foot on the gas pedal that makes me concerned about getting pulled over.

Seth finishes the song on a shout, then laughs as he falls back against his seat. "I haven't heard that song in forever."

"What's it about?" I ask as we fly through wild fields and blue sky.

"Taking what you want, and damn the consequences," he says.

"That doesn't seem very you," I say.

"Well, I was seventeen," Seth says, like it explains everything, and I laugh.

When I look over at him, he's not smiling anymore, and I'm sorry I pointed it out.

He goes quiet for the rest of the drive, only responding to direct questions.

We pull up at Monet's estate in silence. It's made up of Monet's house and gardens, plus a mandatory restaurant and gift shop.

Seth tenses again. "It never goes how you think it will, when you're seventeen, does it?" he asks, staring straight ahead.

That's a massive understatement in my case, but I know what he means. You never end up as the person you think you'll be.

"No," I say quietly. "No, it doesn't."

I unbuckle my seatbelt and open the car door.

"Shall I pick you up in four hours? I imagine you'll want to take your time."

"Pick me up?" I ask dumbly.

"Did you think I was going to make you take a bus back to Amelie's?"

"No, I…" I look toward this world-famous site I've been waiting to see since I knew what painting was, and back at Seth.

I only have a month left with him. Less than a month.

Suddenly, against all my logic and feminist instincts, the most beautiful place in the world looks less appealing.

"You're not coming with me?" I ask.

"You didn't invite me," Seth says, his hand tight on the wheel, even though he's not driving. "I told you I could keep myself busy at the Paris office."

"Do you want to come with me?" I ask, and he's out of the car in a flash.

"Yes," Seth says, locking the car and striding toward the estate. I have to trot to keep up. "Yes, I do."

***

Seth's enough of an art collector to obsess over the way Monet's house is staged. Cozy antique furniture, art on the walls, painting supplies left out as if maybe he just stepped out of the studio. The whole thing feels bright and lit and lived in.

Seth's got a point. I can easily imagine ghosts here. Happy ghosts.

"It's like the whole thing is an art project," Seth says. "I wonder who was in charge of curating it?"

"Well, originally Monet," I say, and Seth rolls his eyes.

I can't be snarky when I step out into the gardens that butt up against Monet's house. The famous Japanese garden with the water lilies is farther on, but I can't imagine it being any better than this. There are roses and vines and sunflowers and more color than I've ever seen in my life. Every breath is laden with the perfume of flowers baked in the hot sun.

And the light. Oh, the light. Everywhere I turn, it brings forth something different, shining through a leaf, highlighting a vibrant petal. The whole thing is a painting made of light and earth.

There's the artificial click of a phone camera. I turn, ready to be annoyed at whoever's looking through a paltry lens when they could be looking at all of this when I see it's Seth.

He's taking a picture of me.

I never thought of Seth as a tourist. Every time I've traveled with him, it's someplace he's been a million times. But of course, there are places he hasn't been, places he's as much a tourist as me.

"Do you want me to take your picture?" I ask.

He snaps another photo of me, then tucks his phone back into his pocket. "Why would I want a picture of me?" he asks simply.

Wandering through the gardens with Seth feels like being in a fairy tale. Talk about not being able to imagine what your life is like at seventeen. I landed in a magical world, next to a prince.

"What are you thinking?" Seth asks, in his beautifully accented voice.

I shake my head. "I don't think I *can* think. It's all too beautiful. Too much."

Seth gestures to a corner of the garden where a man sits with an easel.

"If we ditch some more of Amelie's wedding planning, we could come up again and you could paint."

"Oh Seth. Really? But I couldn't... I'm not... This is for real artists." Artists who haven't forged Monet. Dared to put his name on something he didn't make to fool people who didn't know any better.

"You're a real artist," Seth says quietly. "The way you paint, it makes me think of Vivian LaBlanc."

"Seth..." I say, because the comparison is making me think of Victor's demands, and I don't want those ugly thoughts here, where the grass is sweet underfoot, and the colors are as bright as a stained-glass window when the light shines through.

"I don't know why I do," Seth pushes on. "I don't *get* the impressionists. But the way you paint it feels bright. Alive. Whole. Complete."

I feel like I'm going to cry. He's saying things that can't possibly be true. Because if I'm not a hack, if I can belong with normal, brave-hearted artists who make beauty in a place like this...

If I could have belonged here... how heartbreaking I sold myself so short. I thought the only way in was to pretend to be someone else. And the cruel irony is because I spent so much time pretending to be someone else, I can never actually get in.

That's the only word for it.

Heartbreaking.

Seth takes my hand and gently kisses it.

"Do you want to move on to the lilies? And the bridge?" he asks.

I nod gratefully.

There are more people here. I think we're behind a tour group, and I'm glad because it gives me a chance to pull myself together.

Seth squeezes my hand, then lets it go. I fight the urge to snatch his hand back.

The tour group moves on, giving me a glimpse of the bridge, and my breath catches.

If I thought I was in a painting before...

The way the light hits the lilies floating on the water—even the way the shadow of the bridge falls on the water. Everything is so perfectly choreographed. Another tour group comes along, and Seth gently moves me to the side with a hand on my waist. The tour group murmurs, and snaps pictures, but they're hushed as if we're in a cathedral.

I look up at Seth to see what beautiful thing is catching his art critic's eye in this cool, pearly paradise, but he's looking at me.

His expression is naked, fierce, unguarded.

A man has never looked at me like that. Like he would gladly wake up next to me for a thousand days and a thousand nights, and slay my dragons, and carry my ghosts.

I rise on my toes and kiss him, my palm gentle on his cheek.

He breathes in like he needs every part of me, even my scent, and his mouth opens under my kisses.

Kissing him is...heartbreaking.

You could break your heart on a kiss like this.

He's still holding back, like he's already saying good-bye. I'm so overwhelmed by the beauty around me, by the warmth of his skin beneath my hand, that I can't find my place in the problem. I can't figure out why.

Then I remember. Seth's not going to kiss me until I invite him to. Just like he wasn't going to get out of the car until I invited him.

I know he wants to. His favorite song is about taking. For once, taking what he wants. But it's only a fantasy until I give him the word.

"Seth," I murmur against his lips. "I want you to kiss me."

His hands tighten on my hips.

"Are you sure?" he breathes, and it's more a demand than a question. My stomach flutters.

"I'm sure," I say.

Seth pulls away.

I'm confused until his hand slides through mine and he leads me farther into the deep, cool green of the trees, away from the footbridge and the other travelers.

Seth takes my face in his hands, his eyes traveling to my mouth. He breathes in like it's a hard thing to remember to do.

I'm not sure I'm even breathing. My heart is racing and slowing down all at once, and there are butterflies dancing on my skin.

"Please, Seth," I say. "Kiss me."

He smiles, and there's the familiar secret in the corner of his mouth. I feel closer to knowing that secret than I've ever been.

"You can't control this, Darcy," he says, his voice low and rough. "I'll kiss you when I'm good and ready."

Oh God. Is it wrong to be this turned on in Monet's garden? A little turned on seems like it could be appropriate, bohemian Parisians and all, but this? This dying, crawling-out-of-my-skin, desperate, on-edge want? That seems disrespectful—

Seth kisses me. And he doesn't hold anything back.

***

We lose track of time, which is par for me, but a big deal for Seth. He's casting a spell on us both when he buries his hands in my hair and trails his lips down my neck. When he kisses my eyelids. When his thumb skims the underside of my breast. When he spreads his big hand on the small of my back, like we're dancing again, and he's guiding me closer to him. It's slow and lazy and thorough.

In the distance, another tour group comes and goes. The sunlight moves down my body as I reluctantly pull away, leaning into the shadows. "We should go."

"I'm not ready," Seth says and dips his head to capture my mouth again.

I curl my fingers in his shirt, not sure if I'm stopping him or urging him on or trying to find purchase in a spinning world. "Seth. I need you now. I can't wait."

"You have me now," he says, and kisses me deeply, which is very romantic but entirely misses the point.

"No, I...no." I break away. "I mean I want to sleep with you."

"You sleep with me every night," he says, and I can tell he's proud of his little joke until I skim my thumb where he's hard, and his breath catches.

"Not like this I don't," I say. "But I've wanted to."

"Liar," he says, moving my hand away. "You're trying to wreck me."

I curl my other hand around the back of his neck and rise on my toes to whisper in his ear. "The night you ran into my room? Screaming about bats?"

"Ah yes, one of my more manly moments," he says dryly, casually resting his hands at the flare of my hips, his fingertips warm under the hem of my shirt.

"I was getting myself off, thinking of you," I confess softly into his ear. "How you kiss. How you'd fuck."

His fingers bite into my skin. His eyes are nearly black with want.

"I was almost there from thinking about you, when suddenly there you were, but not for me. Not like I was fantasizing. No," I say, lowering myself from tiptoes and sliding torturously against him as I go. "No, *you* were there for the bats."

For a moment Seth looks at me. Then he throws his head back and laughs, big and deep and joyous.

"Christ, we're idiots," Seth says, smiling down at me as he tucks my hair behind my ear.

I take his hand and start backing toward the bridge area of the garden, pulling him with me. "Come on. There's got to be some charming little B&B in the little town we passed. Or, you know, not charming. I'm flexible."

"You mean a B&B where they'll notice we don't have suitcases, the walls are thin, and they'll hear when you come? No."

I blush and almost trip over a rock. I can whisper filth in his ear without blinking an eye. But when he looks at me matter-of-factly and says *that,* I turn into a mess, my attention skittering from one hot thought to another.

"Maybe I'm quiet," I say. "Dignified. Like a silent film star who dies of consumption in the end, but with perfect lipstick."

Seth's eyes flicker to my mouth. "I'll give you the perfect lipstick."

"Seth, I don't want to go back to the chateau. Nothing against Amelie's…"

He shudders. "God no."

I stop and put my hands on my hips. "Then what are you suggesting? The car?"

A cocky, masculine smile spreads across his face, and he adjusts his glasses.

"Oh no, darling," Seth says. "We're going to Paris."

Chapter Thirteen

Seth

I can feel Darcy watching me as I drive. I don't look back, because if she's having second thoughts, I want to enjoy my denial until we get to Paris.

My heart is pounding. You'd think waiting to make a move until a woman is literally begging in your ear would take the pressure off, but this is Darcy. Mercurial, irreplaceable, addictive Darcy.

When I get up the courage to look over, she's staring at me with such unabashed lust I nearly forget which side of the road I'm supposed to be driving on.

Darcy notices and laughs giddily. "Are we there yet?"

If we're not, I will personally rearrange the geography of France.

***

I get a break from Darcy's undivided attention as we drive into the city.

"Oh, there's the Seine. And look at the little bookstalls on the sidewalk. I mean, don't look, you're driving. It looks like the movies. But better, more real. Oh my fuck. Did you see her shoes?"

I get us a room at a stylish hotel in the heart of the city. It's an old building, but it's been fearlessly remodeled. Glass and chrome butts up against marble and stone in a way that shouldn't work but does.

When we're checking in, Darcy wanders over to investigate some art on the other side of the lobby. I take the opportunity to ask if there are any rooms with a view of the Eiffel Tower.

The answer is yes, for a substantial price increase. I think of Darcy's enthusiasm each time we drove past a landmark and pass over my credit card.

I get our keycards and turn to Darcy.

She's still standing in front of the painting, but there's a man chatting with her now. Black jeans, leather jacket, and the kind of stubble men grow when they're trying to look like they don't care how they look. He's even got a motorcycle helmet dangling from his fingertips. He laughs at something she says, and I'm struck by how right Darcy looks with someone like that. I feel a spurt of possessiveness and reflexively push it down. *Not yours, not yours, not yours.*

Then I remember: *Hell yes, she is.*

For tonight anyway. And if I do this right, maybe a lot longer.

He's asking her something, and Darcy's laughing, shaking her head when I walk up and put my arm around her. When she leans back into me, I feel a spurt of triumph.

"Our room is ready," I say to Darcy, shooting Mr. Motorcycle Jacket a look that says *back off.*

I might be a careful, buttoned-up, non-spontaneous square. But Darcy has fantasies about *me*. So it's time for Tall, Dark, and French to leave.

There's a slight flicker of disappointment in his face letting me know he gets the message.

As he heads off, I guide us to the elevator. As soon as the doors close, I kiss her. It feels like way too long since I've kissed her, and I'm already starving. She's clutching my shirt, her small moan wiping out our surroundings when the elevator dings. I blindly pull her out onto the top floor. I take us toward the wrong room and Darcy has to correct me, with much teasing.

Hell, I even love her teasing. I love—

I break off that thought. Nope. Not going there.

I fiddle with the keycard and swipe us into an elegant room with gray bedding and orange roses and a small mahogany table next to an open window framing the Eiffel Tower.

Well, part of it. I'm not *that* rich.

Darcy crosses to the double-paned window and throws it open.

"Oh come look, Seth. It's all so beautiful."

I watch Darcy, her dark curling hair and the round curve of her cheek framed perfectly in the window. She's so beautiful, it physically hurts.

I don't know what's wrong with me. I've been with beautiful women before. Smart, interesting, gorgeous women. But it's never felt like *this*. I have no idea why.

Well, I have *some* idea why. But I can't go there when she still thinks we're not real. When she's thinking of this as a vacation we'll recover from.

The real reason we're in Paris? Because I need all the help I can get.

The Eiffel Tower lights up, right on cue, the sparkles racing up and down it, and Darcy's gasp of delight makes every penny worth it.

I join her at the window, dropping a kiss at the base of her neck. She's so soft and unguarded there. I wrap my arms around her, and she leans back into me as she takes in the view. If you took a picture of us, you'd think it was a perfect moment. Darcy in my arms, Paris at our feet, and the whole night stretching out before us. Her weight in my arms feels so fundamentally *right*. There's the heady anticipation of what's to come, but it's more than that. Holding her like this feels like coming home.

I don't know if she's ready to let me in.

"I'm glad you're here," I say, and it's true, even if leaving it at that feels wildly inadequate. But I can't say the rest yet. I can't.

I'm always holding myself back with Darcy. I feel like a kid trying to keep the sun from going away at night.

Maybe I can say it, a sliver of it. The Eiffel Tower finishes cascading sparkles, and as I take a deep breath, I can feel her stiffen in my arms.

"Darcy, I—"

"Shh. Let's not talk." She turns, placing a finger on my lips, and I smile, because her finger's still smudged with brilliant emerald green paint from this morning. "Just this once, let's not apologize, or overthink, or be careful, or talk."

"Take what we want, damn the consequences?" I ask, and she nods.

"For one night," Darcy adds hurriedly, like she's worried I'll refuse.

As if I'd refuse her anything tonight. *Or ever*, I think, but I shove the thought away.

I run my hands up her arms. It's not exactly what I want. Certainly not the "one night" bit. But it's close enough.

And it's what Darcy wants.

I kiss her again, this time long and slow, as I back us toward the bed. I'm drunk on her mouth. The future fades under the warmth and softness, the lemony scent of her, the salt of her skin. She kisses me back, hard, her fingers sinking into my hair so tight it almost hurts. Maybe I'm not the only one who's been holding back.

Please let me not be the only one.

Darcy shoves me back on the bed and straddles me, fumbling with my shirt, her hands shaking, her delicious weight stealing my ability to think.

She gets my shirt off and sighs like she's seeing something beautiful, running her hands up my chest, which is nice. Except there are more important things we could be doing right now.

Like getting her out of *her* shirt. But then she's kissing me, and it's kind of blowing my mind she wants me this much. I roll us over, and her gray eyes spark with surprise, then desire as I cage her in. *Mine*.

It's a good thing she said no talking because the things I'm thinking are not progressive, one-night-stand thoughts. I kiss her lips, her neck, the place where her t-shirt has slipped off her shoulder. I bite her nipple through the thin fabric of her t-shirt and feel like a god when she roils under me, restless like the sea.

I trace the line of bare skin between her t-shirt and her jeans, and I know I'm doing good work by the way she sucks in her breath.

It takes half a second to get her pants off, but it feels like forever. Her shirt takes longer since we're both trying to do it at the same time, and it's a temporary tangle of hands and fabric and elbows. Then her shirt flies across the room, and I'm staring down at the most beautiful, gorgeous woman in all of creation. She's soft everywhere, her cheeks flushed, her lips swollen, her curls a wild mess from my hands. I cup her sex, watching the way her breath catches and her lips part.

I should go slow, but after two fucking years, Darcy's in my bed, and I'm losing my mind. My fingers are quick and sure as I get her out of the lacy scrap of a bra with more colors than I knew came on a single undergarment.

When I peel off her underwear—electric pink—and give a gentle, experimental lick, she arcs off the bed.

"*Mr. Moreau.*"

I freeze. Oh God. She's killing me. She wants me to stop *now*? When she's wet and naked in my arms? Dammit, I rushed, I should have gone slower, she seemed like... but that's always been our sign the other person is going too far, and she just gave it to me, loud and clear.

I ease off her and press my forehead into the comforter. I breathe deep, trying to get my body under control.

Fuck. I hope this hotel has really, *really* cold showers.

The bed shifts as Darcy half sits up. "Why did you stop?"

I look up, and bloody hell, she's a vision. Hair wild, breasts bare, looking at me with... somewhat inexplicable irritation.

"You said... It's how we always tell each other when we're going too far," I say.

She blinks. "You mean... when you would say Miss Smith, it meant you wanted me to stop?"

I nod.

"Oops."

I sit up. "Wait. What did you think it meant?"

"I thought it meant we were daring each other to go on. But we never had the guts to."

"So...to be clear," I say. "You don't want me to stop."

Darcy shakes her head so vigorously her curls fly through the air.

"You want me—you're daring me—to do this," I say, bringing my fingers back to her.

"Begging, if we're being accurate," she says, her voice thick with want as she watches me spread her.

Oh thank God. I fall on her, losing myself in her heat and wet and softness, and how badly she wants me, because she's daring me to go on, and she's moaning, her hand seizing in my hair, she's almost there, almost...

I lift my head. "That time, after the gallery opening, when we'd had too much wine, and you were in a black velvet thing with no back, and I told you that you were beautiful, and you said Mr.

Moreau…" I know this is a *very* inopportune time to be asking, but I can't stop myself.

"I wanted you to keep going. To tell me I was the most beautiful woman there."

"You were."

Darcy gives a husky, helpless laugh. "There was a literal supermodel at that party."

"Was there?" I nip at her hip, and she gasps.

"I wore that dress to every gallery opening we went to that year. You never said I was beautiful again. Ever."

"You told me you didn't want me to. At least, that's what I thought," I amend.

I lower my mouth to her clit, but another thought pops into my head. "During the Foran deal, when I lost my temper and told you I expected more from you. Then you tried to quit, and I said I'd tie you to the desk before I let you leave because we were the kind of people who fixed our mistakes. I was being an ass. And you looked at me and said *Mr. Moreau* and walked out in those pointy high-heels."

"I wanted you to fuck me on your desk," she moans, and I almost lose control.

I should stop asking questions, but it's addictive, like picking at a snagged thread until the whole thing unravels and there's nothing left for either of us to hide behind. "The time you called in sick, and you sounded like death, and I asked if you had the medicine you needed."

She's quiet for a moment, then props herself up on her elbows to look at me. "I'd been dumped, and I got drunk. Then I got the flu on top of the hangover. It was the worst twenty-four hours of my life, and I wanted you to tell me everything was going to be ok."

"Oh. Oh, love. I—"

Her hand tunnels through my hair and grips the back of my neck. "Not that I don't appreciate your emotional intelligence, but for God's sake touch me now."

So I do, over and over again, until Darcy's shattering under my mouth and tensing around my fingers. I kiss her through the aftershocks, then crawl up the bed until I'm next to her.

Darcy throws an arm over her eyes. "That…wow. Ok."

I half laugh and pull her arm away from her face. "We're not done yet."

Darcy gives me a wicked grin. "Oh no, did you want something too? 'Cause I think I'm done for the night."

I dive on her, and she laughs. I'm not sure if we're kissing or tickling or wrestling or what, but she's lazy and satisfied, whereas I am horny and motivated, so it ends with her pinned under me, smiling up at me like the cat who swallowed the cream. God, she's beautiful. I'm leaning down to kiss her again when something flickers across her face.

"What?" I ask. "What is it?"

"It's nothing," Darcy tries to duck her head. But we're almost as close as two people can be—almost—and there's nowhere for her to hide.

"Darcy."

"I'm … embarrassed. All those times I thought you were daring me on, and you were really saying 'No, please stop.'"

"To keep my sanity," I say, trailing my mouth over her temple. "If I could have…if I wasn't your boss…" I kiss her mouth, sweet and chaste, which is pretty ironic when my cock is heavy between her legs. "You make it very hard not to want you, Darcy Sherwood."

She takes my face and rises to kiss me. She's doing to my mouth what I was doing between her legs, and before the kiss is over I'm grabbing blindly for a condom in the bedside table. Then I remember this isn't my condo, and there aren't any there. I leave Darcy and grab a condom from my wallet, stripping my pants off and sheathing myself before Darcy has time to do more than shift her hips in the sheets. Then I'm on her, kissing her again.

I'd be nervous if I weren't so fucking desperate.

She breaks away from my lips. "Those times I spilled coffee on you and tried to dry you off?"

I kiss the corner of her mouth. "I can't think when you touch me."

"Interesting." Darcy grips my cock, and my world loses focus under the intense pleasure of it. "Yes, I can see that."

I'm having trouble listening. I need to be in her. *Now.*

"The time I tried to tell you how to win that girl back," Darcy says.

"I didn't want her back." *She wasn't you.*

I slide into Darcy, liking the way she tenses, then relaxes, rolling her hips and clenching in a way which has me shuddering. Her eyes are focused on me, intense, cataloging every moan and tense and shudder she wrings out of me. I know because I'm doing the same thing with her.

"That time," Darcy pants, "when you told me not to talk about the guy I was dating at work. You said it was unprofessional."

I thrust into her. "I wanted you for myself. Now I have you."

She rolls us until she's on top, her dark hair falling in a curtain around us. "That's debatable."

"No," I say, pulling her down to me, gripping her ass. "It's not." Then I'm kissing her and she's moving against me and any pretense at banter fades away into unrelenting, all-consuming pleasure.

When Darcy finally comes around me, burying her head in my neck, her hands knotted in the bedsheets beside my head, I follow, breaking apart in her waves.

Chapter Fourteen

Darcy

A car honks, and a morning breeze blows over my naked shoulder. I burrow under the covers and scooch closer to Seth's heat. It's more than the warmth. I'm like a magnet, going where I'm supposed to be.

"Cold?" he says, his voice low and gruff in the morning. It's both incredibly soothing and arousing. I roll to face him and reluctantly open my eyes.

"Why did we leave the window open?" I grumble.

"I believe you were swept away in the romance of it all."

I bite back a smile. "Well, aren't we full of ourselves."

"I meant Paris."

I laugh, which draws out a lazy smile from him.

"Actually," Seth says, rolling away from me and reaching for his glasses, "I have been a bit remiss in that department. What do you say we plan a night when we get back to New York? Dinner somewhere where the plates are tiny. Broadway. The works."

His voice is casual, but he's taking way too long to put on his glasses. This matters to him.

I feel like I'm too close to the edge of a cliff. Seth Moreau is asking me out on a date. For when we get back to New York.

But I can't. I have to vanish. I have to disappear so Victor can't hurt me. I need to tell Seth no, tell him what we're doing can only last until our vacation ends.

I can't make my mouth form the words. My heart thuds, heavy, like exhausted feet at the end of a marathon.

I'm so tired of hiding. Tired of living half a life. Tired of not getting to have real friends, let alone a real relationship.

"You don't like tiny plates. Or Broadway," I stall.

He looks over his shoulder at me, his grin crooked. "You do."

"Oh."

Seth leans over and cups my cheek, his eyes brilliant behind his glasses. "I'm wooing you."

Oh. Why is this so hard? Why does he have to be like this?

Butterflies swarm my stomach, even as my heart feels full enough to crack. I've been resisting Seth for years. Walking away at the end of the month should be a cinch.

But resisting is a team effort, with us. Now he's not holding up his end of our invisible deal—now he's saying he wants me, and is *wooing* me—I'm crumbling fast.

My hand comes up to caress his cheek, so we're sitting there like mirror images. His stubble is rough on my hand.

"It's ok, Darcy," he says gently.

I close my eyes against the stinging threat of tears.

"Do you need more from me or less?" Seth asks, and there's an urgent thread running through his voice. "I can do either, Darcy. I can pull back and wait. We can get coffee. Watch TV. Or we can go bigger. A weekend upstate. I can tell you... Well, you should probably confirm you don't want to go slow before I finish that sentence."

"Seth..."

He looks down and rubs a thumb over my cheekbone. "Or if it's no... I wouldn't like it, but I'd understand. Well, no, I wouldn't. But I'd respect it."

His forehead drops to mine. "Tell me what you need from me, Darcy, and I'll give it."

You. The thought comes instinctively, upending everything I thought I knew.

I thought I wanted Seth but *needed* to be safe from my past. But what I feel for the man across from me is more than want. I've never felt so hooked on another human being.

His jaw is tight, waiting for my answer.

I bite my lip, and he surprises me by reaching out and running the pad of his thumb along my lip, caressing it.

"It drives me crazy when you do this," Seth says.

I blink. "What? Bite my lip?"

"I need to know what you're thinking. I need to kiss you. I can never do either." He says it with such simple clarity, I know he's been thinking it for a long time.

I had no idea. And that's the thing that does it. I can't walk away from all the things I still need to know about him. Even if it means bringing him closer to all the things he'll hopefully never know about me.

My brain starts whirring. If I do it right, there might be more than one way to be safe. It's always better to cut ties with your blackmailer. But the other option is working with him— long enough to figure out a way to beat him.

One more painting will buy Victor's silence for a while at least. Maybe by the time he demands another one, I'll have enough dirt on him, enough power to refuse for good.

Without running. Without hiding. Without giving up Seth.

I kiss Seth. I'm violent in my kiss, biting his lip, scraping my nails over his back.

He's tender in his.

I break away to look him in the eye. He's oddly imposing for a naked man in spectacles.

"Yes, Seth. I would love to go on a date with you."

His fingers tighten on my waist, and it's a wonderful feeling.

"I'd love—" I start, and he stills. "I'd love to be wooed by you," I finish.

He relaxes. "I can do that."

He kisses me, and his kisses are bright, joyful, playful.

I can't believe how fundamentally I've shifted my world. It doesn't feel real.

I can have the man I want. I can build the life I want.

All I have to do is one last fake.

***

We linger in Paris as long as we can. Croissants and the Louvre with Seth is apparently my perfect morning. But we have to go back.

The sky is crisp as we drive. Clear, beautiful white light bathes the world around us as we leave Paris and the grayer suburbs surrounding it, driving through hills and fields that still have a bit of wild in them.

The idea of keeping Seth is a gloriously exhilarating rush. But what I'm going to have to do to keep him sits heavy in my stomach.

I roll my head to look at Seth, calmly capable in a white shirt, focused on the road ahead.

I never have to worry about anything when I'm with him. Except being good enough to keep him.

"Why do you hate Victor?" I ask.

His jaw goes tense, and his hands tighten on the steering wheel. "Why do you want to know?" His voice is cold.

Because I want to know who I'm up against.

"Because it matters to you," I say instead.

"Lots of things matter to me," he says mulishly. "Let's talk about the undervaluing of living artists, and how that means we're robbed of the art they would make if they weren't working day jobs because everyone wants a piece of the dead artists we've literally already lost."

"Seth. You know what I mean."

He doesn't say anything.

I purse my lips and look ahead. "If you can hate someone you love so much you cut off contact, I want to know why. If we're… whatever we are… it's relevant."

He sighs. "Darcy, you'd never do what he did."

I bite my lip. Sometimes I *helped* Victor do what he did. "Humor me?"

Seth looks ahead. Finally, he sighs.

"I guess, in a weird way, I owe him for meeting you," he says.

A chill goes down my spine. "What?"

"It was two years ago. The day I met you. There'd been some rumblings in the art world about too many forgeries on the market. There's always some, but there were a lot. They were damn convincing."

"You don't say."

"You don't get it, Darcy, these were good. Really, really good. I saw one, once, at Victor's." He drums his fingers on the steering wheel. "He was hosting this cocktail party, and my date and I wandered into his study. That's when I saw it. One of Monet's water lily paintings. A late one, from when his vision was going. It was so loose and soft, it was almost a feeling. And there it was, on Victor's desk."

I look down at my hands. I remember that painting. I hadn't wanted to hand it over by the time I finished it, I loved it so much.

"Victor was authenticating it. It was so good he probably would have screwed up and authenticated it, but my date was an art authenticator too, for insurance companies. She figured out it was a fake."

"How?" I ask indignantly, before I remember that's not the part of the story I'm supposed to be indignant about.

But still. It was a damn good forgery.

"It was a feeling," Seth says. "She looked at it and knew it was wrong. It wasn't until months later, after we'd stopped dating, she figured it out. The trees and the water lilies were from different seasons. They never would have both looked like that at the same time. You'd only paint it that way if you were taking the most beautiful pieces of Monet's paintings, instead of painting from the garden itself."

"Stupid mistake," I say bitterly.

"If you're trying not to get caught stealing, absolutely. If you're trying to make something beautiful... that's what the impressionists did, right? They took the feeling of a place, not the literal truth of it."

I don't let myself look at him. It feels like I'm being seen for the first time in my life, and my chest feels full and tight. But I know if he ever actually does see that part of me, I'll lose everything.

"I tried to buy it," Seth admits.

"What?"

"After I knew it was a forgery. It wasn't worth real money then, and I liked it. I felt this wistful, beautiful peace when I looked at it. But Victor wouldn't sell. He was adamant if I bought a forged painting, even if I told everyone it was forged, it would still make me look suspicious. I thought he was being paranoid, but..." He rolls his shoulders and shakes his neck out like this next part is the hardest to tell.

"What?"

"It felt good to have him looking out for me like that. He hadn't done it in a long time." He says it quietly, like he's ashamed of himself. Like wanting to trust someone you love is a character flaw.

I never thought I was stealing more than money with the forgeries. But now I'm realizing how naive—how selfish—it was to think that.

"What does this have to do with why you hate Victor?" I ask.

"The forgeries attracted a lot of attention, partly because they were appearing at the same time famous paintings were being stolen. There was a rash of robberies in private collections and small museums. Then these paintings would show up on the black market, and people would assume they were buying the real thing. When they found out it wasn't the real thing, if they ever did, they had nowhere to go, because they'd have to admit they'd tried to buy a stolen painting."

I blink. I vaguely remembered stories about robberies around that time, but I hadn't paid enough attention to tie it to the works I was forging.

"There was a lot of pressure from insurance companies, from the FBI, from everyone, to find who was making these forgeries, because the trail on the robberies was going cold, and the forgeries were their best lead."

"But what if the forger was only making use of the situation to sell paintings to people who couldn't turn them in?" I ask, trying to sound uninterested.

"Yeah, that's what most people who followed the case think now," Seth says. "There was this big art bust, and they raided a whole office filled with forgeries. They caught some of the forgers, but not all of them. Not the best one. The forgeries stopped a long time ago, but the robberies continued. So yeah, probably no connection."

My mouth feels dry. The raid he's talking about has to be the one I almost walked straight into, on the day I met Seth. I can still remember those flashing lights. The uniforms going in and out of the building. The day the risk I was running became too big to ignore.

"What does this have to do with Victor?" I ask again.

Seth briefly takes his eyes away from the road and looks at me. "Don't make me tell you this, Darcy. Because if I tell you this, I need you to keep the secret. I hate him, but he's my brother, and I can't... So are you sure you want to know?"

I bite my lip. There's a part of me that wants to put my hands over my ears and run away. But I need all the information I can get.

And, surprisingly more important, I need Seth not to be alone with this.

"I'm sure." I put a hand on his thigh. "I'm good at keeping secrets."

"Right. Ok." Seth's thigh tenses under my hand, like this is hard to say. "Well, Victor called me and said he'd been paranoid. Said he was in the neighborhood for a meeting with a friend, and he'd give me the painting if I could stop by the friend's office in the next half hour. We'd left it on kind of a weird note, after the cocktail party. No one likes being professionally shown up by their little brother's date. I took it for the olive branch it was and headed over. But the subway was a mess, and I was running late when I bumped into you. And, well... you remember."

"Of course." I remember my heart pounding so hard it felt like it would bruise the inside of my chest as I fled until Seth accidentally saved me. But he's saying I'm the one who saved *him*. "You asked me if I was looking for a job. I said yes."

"But you wanted to do the job interview right then. I was pretty sure I'd already missed Victor. So I sent him an apology text and said I'd buy him a drink to make up for it. Then we did your interview over coffee, and you came to see the office. I didn't think anything else of it until I got home and checked the news."

His knuckles are white on the wheel. "The office they raided was where I was supposed to meet Victor. I grabbed my phone to call him. I thought the criminal must be his friend who had the office, that Victor must be feeling so betrayed. I wondered if the FBI had thought the worst when they saw Victor there with a forged Monet. I panicked, thinking he'd been accidentally implicated because he was trying to do a nice thing for me. But the news said no one was in the office with the paintings other than a few former art students. No other civilians had come in all day. I watched them carry out Victor's fake Monet on the news. The man carrying it was wearing blue rubber gloves, and they clashed with the blue on the painting."

I feel sick. "Maybe Victor dropped it off the day before. Maybe he wasn't trying to—"

"I had ten missed texts on my phone, asking where I was. Saying Victor was there, waiting for me. Saying I better show up, or else." Seth's jaw clenches. "But he wasn't there. The news said he wasn't there. But he wanted *me* there. He wanted *me* there when the place was being raided, asking about a forged painting I was there to pick up."

I feel white-hot blinding rage. Seth could have ended up in prison. Because Victor needed a fall guy.

"I'm going to kill him."

Seth shakes his head. "This is why I didn't want to tell you. He probably knew no charge against me would stick. I don't even deal with art that old. My finances are clean. I have no motive. The only reason anyone knew the painting was a forgery was because of me."

"Which is why he tried to discredit you." I slam my hand against the side of the door. "I am going to murder him."

For the first time since we started this subject, Seth cracks a smile. "Feeling a little protective there?"

"Damn right. He shouldn't have… Not to you." Not to someone good. We only dragged other bad people down with us. That was the deal. "I never thought he'd do something like this," I mutter into my palm.

Seth's eyes sharpen. "You say that like you've known him longer than this trip."

Shit. I'm falling apart. I need to get control of my emotions *now*. I need to give Seth something he'll believe.

I look away. "I didn't realize it before, but I met him at a college art show. You meet a lot of people, and you're trying so hard to make connections… I wouldn't have remembered, except he was younger than most of the other art dealers who came. He felt a little slimy."

Seth laughs, delighted. "Really? You thought he was slimy? Most women think he's charming." He reaches over and rubs the back of my neck affectionately. "Good for you."

I smile weakly. I wish I'd thought Victor was slimy. I wish it so badly I'd cut off a toe, to be able to go back in time and grab myself and say *No, don't trust him, not every opportunity is a good one, get out fast.*

"Why don't you turn him in?" I ask. "He couldn't have known to set you up if he wasn't running the forgery ring. Or somehow connected."

Seth pulls his hand from my neck. "He's my brother."

"But—"

"He's my brother, Darcy. I can't trust him. I can't forgive him. But I can't hurt him like that. Not for anything."

I feel a well of frustrated tenderness. Because Seth could make everything better for us if he turned his brother in.

But I love this is who Seth is. I thought I had to worry about Seth turning his back on me the way he turned it on Victor.

Instead, I learned that even if I literally frame him for a crime he didn't commit, there's a part of him that would resist hurting me.

He shouldn't go admitting that to people. I want to shield him from the world.

"Does Amelie know?" I ask.

Seth shrugs one shoulder. "She knows the broad outlines. Victor was selfish and put me in a situation where I could have been arrested and had my entire career ruined. She doesn't know the details."

"But if she knew, surely she wouldn't give everything to Victor. You wouldn't have to…" I hold my left hand and wiggle my ring finger.

"I thought of that. But what if she turns him in?" Seth asks reasonably.

I blink. "Wouldn't want that."

He nods like he's glad I understand.

Dear God. I'm fucking a saint.

Seth blows out a sigh. "God, it feels good to tell someone. I haven't told anyone about it. Not even my therapist."

I glance over. "You have a therapist?"

"Had. I was angry last year after Victor… did what he did. I lost decade-long friendships because I couldn't trust people, couldn't talk to them. Dr. Reed did her best, and it was helpful. But there's only so much she could do when I wasn't willing to tell her why I was so angry. She gave me some tools, and a direction to go in. But ultimately it took time."

We're almost to Amelie's. The sun is setting as we make the turn onto her estate. I can't help but think we've spent the last few years as accidental mirror images, both of us reeling from the same FBI raid, both of us unable to have normal friendships because of the secrets we're holding.

The difference is, I did it to myself. Seth's innocent.

We park, and I start to unbuckle when Seth leans over and kisses me, hard. "Is there anything else you want to know?"

I shake my head, my throat tight. He answered the question I hadn't known I was asking.

Are you worth getting back into bed with Victor for?

He starts to pull away, but I grab his collar and kiss him back, hard.

"Is there anything else you want to tell me?" I tease.

But to my surprise, Seth hesitates. Like there *really is* something he wants to tell me.

"Seth. What is it?"

"Nothing. I mean, not nothing…" He shakes his head and gets out of the car. "Forget it."

"What?" I ask, following him up the steps to the house.

"Forget it, Darcy."

I race up to cut him off in front of the door. He's a few steps down from me, which means we're eye to eye. Something about it throws me back to when I first kissed him, during the photo shoot. I feel like Cinderella, standing on the steps with the prince as sunset turns into twilight. But instead of running like hell before he finds out who she really is, I'm lying as fast as I can to hold on.

I know I shouldn't push him. God knows it's the pot calling the kettle black. But I am greedy to know everything I can about this man.

I tuck a strand of hair behind his ear. "You can understand why I'm curious. The last thing you didn't want to tell me was how you almost ended up arrested for art forgery. What's bigger than that?" I ask gently.

He closes his eyes briefly, and there's that old smile in the corner of his mouth. The one he uses when he doesn't want to show me what he's really feeling.

When Seth opens his eyes, they're fierce, focused, and my stomach flips. His attention is so intense, I'm starting to get nervous. "Seth, I—"

"I love you."

My world stops. "What?"

"I love you, Darcy. I know it's too soon, which is why I wasn't going to tell you. But you asked if there was anything else I wanted to tell you. So there it is. I'm in love with you, Darcy. I am desperately head over heels for you."

"But…" My heart is racing, scared to believe him. "It's been a month. And that's if you count the pretending. Even less if you count—"

"It's been two years and three months," Seth says steadily. "I'm sure."

I'm giddy and terrified and I can't breathe.

He lifts my hands, kisses them each gently. Then he kisses me, softly.

"I don't expect you to be there yet," Seth says. "But that's where I am. I love you."

Now I begin to let myself believe it—*Seth Moreau loves me*—I can't stop smiling.

Why the hell is the sun setting? I feel like I'm standing in the middle of a million sunrises.

I trace his face in wonder. "Seth, I—"

The door slams open, and we both jump.

"There you are," Amelie says. "Honestly, how long does it take to drive from Paris? I was about to send out the search parties."

Seth's smile is crooked as he answers Amelie, never taking his eyes off mine. "We're not in any rush to get where we're going."

"How very poetic of you," Amelie says dryly. "Unfortunately, dinner is rushing toward the inedible. Love may conquer all, but it can't conquer cold soup."

It's the kind of comment that's been making Seth uncomfortable since we got here, but this time he laughs and kisses Amelie on the cheek, before casually looping his fingers through mine and leading me into the dining room.

I peek back over my shoulder to see if Amelie's noticed the change.

She winks at me.

She looks far too self-satisfied for a woman whose soup is going cold.

***

That night, after dinner, I wait until everyone but Victor has left the room. He's slouched across the table from me. I stand. Somehow he still manages to look like the one in charge, loose and sprawled like a hunting cat.

He raises an eyebrow. "You should scurry off, little Robin, before your fiancé gets jealous. Although how jealous he'll be once we leave France and he finds out who you truly are…"

"I'll do it." I grip the chair in front of me for support.

Victor's face spreads in a genuine smile. "Wonderful. I knew you'd come around. I expect it in four days."

I wince. That's a nearly impossible deadline, especially when you factor in the gamut of activities Amelie has planned. But I don't protest. I want this over with as soon as possible.

I keep my voice low as I ask, "Which of Vivian LaBlanc's paintings am I replicating?" Sound carries in this house.

Victor's smile turns into a smirk. "Oh no. You're not replicating a painting. You're creating an original. A brand-new Vivian LaBlanc discovered in her hometown. The world will go wild. No hiding in the shadows for this one."

Fuck. He was serious about that part.

I run my hands along the back of the chair, trying to channel Amelie's unbothered elegance. "With something so high profile, out in the open… They'll run tests. We'll get caught."

"We won't get caught. Because I'm not selling it. I'm giving it to my beloved aunt. Who will be so grateful and impressed, she'll know exactly who should inherit our priceless family art collection." He stands. "Honestly, you've let your criminal instincts go. Practice makes perfect, dear."

What if his plan works? What if a new LaBlanc sways Amelie?

I hadn't thought it was possible when Victor first proposed it. But I just found out Seth almost walked into an FBI raid because he wanted a forged Monet.

He doesn't even *like* Monet. This family is not exactly rational when it comes to art.

"It won't work," I bluff. "Amelie won't give in that easily." Forging again is one thing. Helping Victor steal the estate from Seth is another.

"That's none of your concern." Victor heads toward the door. "I expect you in my room, four nights from now, with the LaBlanc. If it's not there by midnight, you know exactly what's going to happen."

My mind is racing. I need a million things—the seed of a plan is beginning to form—but the first is more time.

I don't like doing it this way, but...

"I need you to get me out of wedding planning activities with Amelie for the next four days. Which means I need you to keep Seth busy."

He turns around in the doorframe, annoyed. "*Someone's* gotten needy in the past two years."

"Someone's gotten careful. You want a LaBlanc, this is how you get it."

I hold my breath, trying to look strong. Uncompromising.

Trying to look like Seth when he's about to walk out on a million-dollar deal because it's not a two-million-dollar one.

Victor gives an exaggerated sigh. "Fine. I'll keep them busy. But you better not be using the time to plan something."

I hold my hands up in surrender. "I swear. I'll only be painting."

He gives me a suspicious look, then nods once and leaves.

I lower my hands. The plan I'm forming is a long shot. More than a long shot. It's a long shot, at a zigzagging target, when there's a horde of zombies chasing you, and you only have one arrow.

I leave the dining room and head upstairs to our bedroom.

I've spent the last two years avoiding shots like that.

But for Seth? For this good and decent man with the wicked smile and a quiet bravery I didn't think existed outside of fairy tales?

I hesitate with my hand on the antique doorknob.

For Seth, I can take the shot.

Then I go inside, to the man who loves me, and love him until I am strong enough to pull this off.

Chapter Fifteen

Seth

For unknown reasons, I am standing in a bridal boutique with my brother, surrounded by wedding dresses. There's so much white in here, it's like a ski trip to the Alps but more expensive.

I still don't get why Victor and I are here with Amelie, instead of Darcy and Barbie. It's hardly a conventional wedding, but normally the bride at least picks her own *dress*. But Barbie's got food poisoning, although I don't know how since we've all been eating the same thing. Darcy volunteered to stay behind with her, and Victor volunteered us for dress shopping, and neither of them would budge, despite anything Amelie or I said. It's so odd, I'd suspect the three of them of being up to something if it weren't for the death glares Darcy was giving Victor, and the sound of Barbie puking into a nineteenth-century porcelain umbrella stand in the hallway.

So here I am, surrounded by lace and tulle and silk and ribbons and more tulle for good measure, while a befuddled sales associate named Chris looks from me to Victor to Amelie and back again. Chris is elegantly dressed in asymmetrical androgynous clothing and looks tempted to call the police.

"You want two dresses. For a double wedding in less than three weeks. And you want to buy them *without the brides*."

Amelie has the grace to look ashamed. Victor's futzing with his phone.

Chris is waiting for an answer.

"Er. Yes?" I say.

"I see. Is there a *reason* they can't be here?" Chris's tone suggests things like child brides, kidnapping, and/or brainwashing.

"I could have you fired—" Victor starts, but I step on his foot.

"They have food poisoning," I say. "But we're on a time crunch. As you said, less than three weeks."

"Hmmm," Chris says noncommittally. "What sizes?"

Shit. Victor and I look at each other, then hastily look away.

"Tall," Victor says at the same time I say, "short."

Chris looks at Amelie. "I fit you in because Jane's my favorite photographer and she asked me to, but I swear to God if you do not know the size dress you're looking for, I will kick you out of the store right this second."

Amelie rattles off a string of measurements, and Chris nods once, looking relieved, before leading us to the back of the shop. "I think we can do that. We mostly only carry sample sizes in-store, but it sounds like this Barbie—" the name is said with French distaste— "will fit the dresses sized to the models for last month's show."

Chris snaps at Victor and points to a rack. "You look here."

Chris looks at me. "Your Darcy might fit sample sizes, but when you're short and curvy tailoring is a must, and you don't have that luxury. Stick to the stretchy fabrics."

Chris says *stretchy fabrics* the way someone else might say *dirty gym shorts.*

Chris parks me in front of a rack and disappears with Amelie to talk veils.

"What a waste of time," Victor mutters. "Barbie won't wear a veil."

I agree, but I'm surprised Victor pays enough attention to Barbie to know that.

I glance over to see Victor groping the dresses. "What the *hell* are you doing?"

"Looking for pockets. Barbie only wears things with pockets."

See, I would have said she only wears things with spandex and animal prints, but apparently Barbie is more practical than I gave her credit for.

"Damnit. None of these dresses have pockets."

"It's a wedding." I flip through my rack. I'm sympathetic to Barbie's pocket needs, but I also want to get out of this store and back to Darcy as fast as possible. "She's not going to need her wallet. Besides, anything she needs, you can put in your pocket."

"She never lets me carry her gun," Victor says.

"*What?*" I yelp, whirling to look at him. "*It's real?*"

Victor scowls. "Of course it's real. Why the hell would she want a fake gun?"

"How did she... there's customs. Airport security. I..." I trail off. My elderly aunt and the woman I love have been staying under the same roof as a woman with a gun, and a man who drives that woman to violence on a semi-regular basis.

The end of the month cannot come soon enough.

Victor shrugs, unconcerned. "I assume there were blowjobs involved."

"You're not even *trying* to pretend you love her," I say.

For some reason that gets under Victor's skin.

"At least I know she's taking her cut and leaving when this is all over," Victor hisses. "That's more honest than anything you and Darcy have."

"What's that supposed to mean?" My voice is cold.

We stare each other down.

Victor's the one who looks away. "Nothing."

We go back to flipping through wedding dresses. I'm not seeing them until my fingers catch a surprising texture.

I hold out the dress to look at it. It's a white velvet wrap dress with an uneven hemline and vaguely gothic white lace trimming. Tiny embroidered burgundy flowers with green leaves are scattered sporadically around the skirt to keep the whole thing looking a little fresh, a little wild.

I've never imagined a woman I'd marry wearing anything like this. But it's perfect for Darcy.

Not that we're getting married.

I take it off the rack, smiling like an idiot, at the same time Victor says, "Fuck it," and grabs a dress at random.

When he looks at me, he winces. "Jesus."

"Fuck you. She'll love this dress. It's not my fault you don't have anything Barbie wants."

"Because none of them have pockets," Victor huffs. He throws a dress worth thousands of dollars on the ground and storms out.

Then, because he's a dramatic piece of shit, he stops a few steps from the door, stalks back to me, and jabs a finger at me. "You'd think after what I did to you, you'd be less of a goddamn mark. But you'll believe anything she fucking says."

I grab for him, but the dress in my hand slows me down, and Victor skips back, ducking under tulle and dodging around racks of dresses. The bell rings as the shop door opens, followed by a slam telling me he's made his escape.

Chris and Amelie emerge from the racks, holding a handful of veils.

"What was that about?" Chris asks, before spotting the dress on the floor and gasping in horror.

"We'll take that one," I say hurriedly. "And this one."

I hold up Darcy's dress.

Chris blinks. "Really? You don't strike me as a risk-taker."

"It's not for me," I say. Chris is possibly the worst salesperson I've ever met.

Chris and Amelie pick a retro fingertip veil for Darcy.

I pick the biggest, fluffiest, over-the-top veil for Barbie, and make it clear it's what Victor wanted.

***

The wedding dress boutique is not the weirdest outing I go on with Victor over the next few days. Whatever Amelie comes up with, Victor finds a way for it to end with me and him doing it together, while Darcy and Barbie stay home. When I broach the possibility he might be up to something with Amelie, she pushes my concerns aside and says he's probably trying to repair our relationship.

I try not to scoff too audibly.

Then there's Darcy. I try not to let the fact she hasn't said *I love you* back bother me. Except she hasn't even said she *likes* me. And she's frustratingly vague about what she's been doing when I've been with Victor and Amelie.

I can count on one hand the number of times Darcy has been vague. One of those times, it turned out she was married.

When she *is* with me, she walks around in a daze like she's seeing things that aren't there. The only time she doesn't shut me out is when we're having sex, and then she focuses with such intensity, it's like one of us is going off to war, and she's trying to memorize me, in case we never see each other again.

I can't tell which one of us she thinks is leaving.

At least I know she's leaving when this is over. That's what Victor said. Does he know something about Darcy I don't?

No. Obviously not. She can't stand him. Even if she were leaving, Victor wouldn't know anything about it.

On the third night, Darcy stays out until one in the morning. When she comes to me at night, there are streaks of color under her fingernails. I'm half asleep as I kiss each finger.

"Painting, love?"

She retracts her nails into fists and rolls away from me. "Why would I be painting? It's the middle of the night."

I'm about to call her on her bullshit, but I can't think of a reason for her to be lying, and I was dead asleep before she crawled into bed, so maybe I am dreaming.

***

The next morning, when she's still asleep, I put on my glasses and check her nails. They're perfectly clean. No color anywhere.

I roll out of bed and dress, unable to shake the mounting unease. It feels like Darcy's keeping a secret from me. But that makes no sense.

I can't wait for this whole thing to be over. To be home, with Darcy, dating like normal people, instead of elaborately planning a fake wedding for Amelie's benefit.

I stop midway through buttoning up my shirt, as a new problem occurs to me. If this thing with Darcy lasts... If Darcy eventually loves me back, and we decide...

How the hell would I ever explain a real wedding to Amelie?

"You missed a button, handsome," Darcy says, her smile lazy. A sleeping beauty who never needed anyone to wake her up.

"Morning." I walk over and drop a kiss on her snarky, generous mouth.

She parts her lips for me, and when we finish my shirt is entirely unbuttoned.

"There," she says smugly. "I fixed it."

I laugh, and her face lights up with delight before turning serious.

"What is it?" I ask. The question feels urgent because I *know* something's wrong between us. I know it the way I know what art will grab people by the heart and shake them into paying attention, and which art will gather dust in someone's basement.

She chews her lip, and I rub her upper arms.

Tell me, Darcy. Tell me what it is.

"It's nothing," she says. I sigh and start to stand, turning away to button my shirt.

Darcy catches my wrist. "Do you trust me, Seth?"

"Of course," I say, and she breathes a sigh of relief, closing her eyes. She still looks unsure, so I add, "I trust you as much as I trust my family."

Her eyes fly open. Those big gray eyes pierce me, and for a second it's like I can't breathe. I can't shake the feeling we're in the eye of a storm, and everything's going to come crashing down around us.

She forces a smile, and the feeling passes. "Well, that's enough for me." With that cryptic comment, she rises from the bed, kisses me on the cheek, and heads toward the shower.

I don't see her again all day.

Chapter Sixteen

Darcy

It's 4:05 p.m. when I finish the Vivian LaBlanc. I blow on my hands for warmth. I've taken over a corner of the broken-window room upstairs as my studio. The door locks, no one comes up here, and I have a clear view of the driveway from the window, so I can see when Seth and the others are returning for the day.

In some ways, this is the hardest forgery I've ever done. Trying to avoid arousing Seth and Amelie's suspicions, trying to stay anonymous when I venture into town for supplies, or to the roads Vivian LaBlanc would have walked down.

In other ways, it's incredibly easy. I'm surrounded by the landscape that created her. I mix my paint with dirt from behind her house. Instead of mimicking an old canvas, I buy a nearly old enough painting from the dustbin at the back of an antique store, and after coating it with a toxic-smelling paste to weaken the paint, I scrape the paint off the canvas. It's the ugliest painting of a bowl of fruit I've ever seen, but I still feel bad about it. Someone long dead made this, or tried to, and I'm scraping what could be the last record of their creativity off the face of the earth.

But this might be the only way to save Seth and me, so I whisper an apology to the long-dead artist and finish scraping.

The biggest difference between this and every other forgery I've ever done?

I'm trying to get caught.

Not right away. I need the painting to pass muster with Victor but stick out like a sore thumb to a real expert. Thanks to Seth, I know I did that once before. Now I need to do it on purpose.

I survey my work. I've picked the woods behind the house Vivian grew up in. It's a sight anyone who's read books on Vivian, or been to her house, would recognize. We have sketches she's made of those woods, but no paintings.

None until this.

As with other LaBlancs, I've painted a woman in motion. She's running through the forest, her skirts flashing orange around her ankles, chased by a man. You can't tell from his shadow if she's being hunted or courted, but if you look at the fierce look of triumph on her face, you can tell she's winning.

The brushstrokes, the subject matter, the lighting, that lie of a signature *Maurice Robinson*: everything is pure LaBlanc.

Except for what I do next.

I flip the painting. LaBlanc always put Robinson's name along the edge of water. Whether a river, or a puddle of rain, or a glass someone was drinking out of. So I've put my Robinson along a stream.

Now I lean in, painting what looks like a soft, blurry reflection of the words into the water. If you haven't studied the signature in a million paintings, this reflection blends into every other reflection in the water. If you have, I'd bet money something about it will snag your brain. And once you look at the reflection, you'll see it's not a reflection at all.

It's a second signature. *Vivian LaBlanc*.

I finish the signature, heart beating fast, and blow on it.

Then I flip the painting right side up again and survey everything I've done.

That will be enough, right?

It has to be.

Now all I need is to figure out how to get Victor exposed trying to pass off this forgery as real in front of Amelie.

I've got some rough ideas. I know I need to get an art expert in the room, and I need to get them in without alerting Victor he's being set up. Seth's an expert in contemporary art, but he doesn't know enough about the impressionists. An insurance investigator would be the most obvious route, but if it goes wrong, I don't want to accidentally set Amelie up to commit insurance fraud.

I go downstairs to grab my laptop and do some more research.

***

"Why are you researching French art fraud stings?" Barbie drawls, and I nearly jump out of my skin, barely keeping myself from slamming the laptop closed.

Don't be suspicious, Darcy. Don't be suspicious.

This is what I get for doing research in Amelie's office. Unfortunately, it's the only room in the whole damn house with a strong enough wi-fi signal to get anything done.

"Oh, you know. Boredom." I make myself stretch casually. "Once you start clicking on Wikipedia links, you end up down some weird rabbit holes."

"Don't I know it," Barbie says, her voice honeyed as always. But there's a sharpness to her eyes I don't like.

What if she reports this back to Victor? What if she and Victor are in cahoots on more than the fiancée scheme?

I didn't think she was, but…

"Do you think criminals research art busts ahead of time? So they don't get caught?" I keep my eyes on her face, watching for her reaction. Any reaction.

Which is how I catch the slightest frown. The smallest tightening at the corners of her mouth.

"I don't know," Barbie says at last. "But I bet cops research every bust that goes right, and every bust that goes wrong, and everyone who gets caught before a bust even has to be made. I wouldn't count on the first page of a Google search to keep me safe if I was deciding whether or not to break the law. The only thing you'll find there is what the reporters know. And that's only the tip of the iceberg."

I blink. It's maybe the sincerest thing I've ever heard Barbie say. "You sound like you know what you're talking about."

And like that she's back to being Barbie. She guffaws. "Oh, bless your heart. No, I don't know nothing about this. My mamma dated a lot of lifers. Do you know when everyone's coming back from picking up the wine?"

I glance at Amelie's ornate gold clock.

Shit. "Looks like they should be home in a half-hour. See you at dinner?"

Barbie pouts at being dismissed, but she takes her cue and leaves me alone in the study.

I listen to her steps fade down the hall, then I dive back into my research.

What reporters know. There's my answer.

Amelie wanted to have a reporter do a write-up on the wedding for the local paper. Rosalind something, her name was.

A quick search gets me a Rosalind Tillion, who does indeed write for the vows section of the local paper if Google translate is to be believed.

I look up her contact information and cross my fingers she's as hungry for a scoop as every other reporter I've talked to at gallery shows.

I head up to my makeshift studio to make the call that will change my life, one way or the other.

My hands are shaking as I dial the number. After several tries landing me in her voicemail, I finally get through to Ms. Tillion.

"*Oui?*" she barks.

"Ms. Tillion, I'm calling about the Moreau weddings in a few weeks. Amelie Moreau said she'd been in touch?"

"Ah. You are the American?" Her accent is thick, but she's way more fluent in English than I am in French. "I will come out for the wedding. If you would like to send me some background information, my email is—"

"I think you should come out tomorrow."

There's a pause. "One meeting is sufficient. It is a brief piece." I can almost hear her saying *You're not as important as you think you are.*

I swallow. I could still get out of this. I could give up now, keep myself safe. But if I do, Seth might lose the Moreau family inheritance, and Amelie will end up with an obvious forgery she might try to insure someday.

"Good-bye, miss," Ms. Tillion says.

"It's not about the weddings," I say in a rush.

"Oh?"

"There's a piece of art that's been…discovered. If you were to come here, to start your piece on the weddings, say, tomorrow…you'd have a big scoop on your hands." I hold my breath, waiting to see if she bites.

"If the piece of art is, as you say, a scoop, why me? Why not another reporter?"

Shit, I should have thought of this.

I pace, trying to channel my character. Outsider fiancée. Doing what she can to fight her way into a family she doesn't belong in, to be with a man she does. "There are members of the family who are…private when it comes to the press. Privacy is of no use in a financial climate like this. But they won't listen to *the American*. So if a reporter they already trust happens to be on site…oops."

In the distance, I can see Seth's car making its way up the drive.

Come on, Ms. Tillion. Shit or get off the pot.

"How do I know this great art find is real?" she asks, still skeptical, but clearly drawn in. "What if you're calling me instead of an art reporter because you want publicity for a work of shaky provenance?"

I punch the air. "You're welcome to bring your own art expert. Say, someone who specializes in local female impressionists from the 1800s."

There's a gasp on the other end of the phone line. "*No*. You can't mean…?"

"I've said too much," I say. "Come tomorrow at ten. Introduce the expert as your assistant when you get here."

"*Oui*," she says faintly, and I hang up.

For a moment I stare down at my phone. I can't quite believe what I've done. I hear the sound of car doors slamming in front of the house.

They're here. I shake my hands out, crack my neck. Any second now, Seth is going to ask to know how my day was.

Bad enough he noticed the paint on my fingers last night.

I take a deep breath and unlock the door.

I've got to lie to Seth for sixteen more hours. Give the painting to Victor, and make sure Victor presents it to Amelie at breakfast right as the reporters arrive at ten a.m.

Hopefully, the expert will expose Victor, and Victor will keep quiet about my involvement, rather than risking me implicating him in everything else we've done.

If he doesn't, I'll deny everything. Then I'll find out what exactly Seth meant when he said, *I trust you like family*.

My stomach cramps. I hope it doesn't come to that. My bravado this morning aside, I don't want to know who Seth would pick.

I leave the room, lock the door behind me, and head downstairs to meet my beautiful fake fiancé and his lying ass of a brother.

***

I'm on edge as I lie in bed, staring up at the ceiling, waiting for Seth to turn off the lights. It's like he caught my case of nerves. He stays up answering work emails he's ignored for weeks, so I lie awake too, reading my novel. Waiting.

I need to get the painting to Victor tonight and get him to hand the painting over at breakfast, or the whole plan crumbles.

"You haven't turned a page in the last ten minutes," Seth says, without taking his eyes off his computer screen.

"It's a good page. Tons of sexy bits."

He smiles, but it doesn't reach his eyes. I glance over at the screen to see what has him so captivated.

He's messaging a woman whose profile picture is gorgeous. Eloise Huntington. It takes me a moment to figure out why the name is familiar.

Then I remember, and it's like someone dropped a brick on my chest.

I sent flowers to her, all those lifetimes ago, when Seth canceled their date. Except it wasn't all that many lifetimes ago if they're still messaging.

Don't be an idiot. Seth said he loves you.

But no matter how many times I tell myself, I can't forget he doesn't know who I really was before he loved me. If tomorrow goes wrong, I'll be asking him to choose between me and his brother.

"Work?" I ask, trying to keep my voice casual.

"Sort of." He closes the laptop, takes off his glasses, and turns off the light. "Telling you everything about Victor the other day got me thinking. I was curious if they ever caught the main forger."

A chill runs through my veins. Eloise must be the art insurance expert. That's so much worse than flirting with an old flame.

Unless he's thinking about turning Victor in?

I turn toward Seth in the dark. "Aren't you worried asking questions like that will put attention on Victor?"

"No. Victor can't paint like that. Whatever he did, or might have done, he's not the forger. Besides, it's only a few questions." He leans over and kisses me good night. It's all I can do not to grab him, and shake him, and tell him to stop asking questions he doesn't want the answer to.

***

It takes forever for Seth's breath to deepen, for him to fall asleep. I check the clock. I'm hours late getting the painting to Victor. It's almost four in the morning. Still, I hesitate.

Now or never, Darcy.

"I'm doing this for us," I whisper, before slipping out of bed. In the dark I throw on a sweater and pants over the t-shirt I've been sleeping in. I slip into the silent hallway and creep upstairs. The key to the broken-window room imprints into my palm, I'm clutching it so hard.

The sound of the key in the lock is crazy loud as I twist it, and then the door creaks as I push it open and step inside. An icy wind blows through the room as I grab the painting and head back to the door.

The sooner I'm done with this, the better.

I step out into the hallway, slowly and carefully shutting the door behind me. I breathe a sigh of relief when it closes without making a sound.

"What are you doing?"

I jump, scream, clap a hand over my mouth to stop the sound.

It's Seth. My body relaxes at the sight of him, and my heart starts to slow before I remember the painting dangling from my fingertips.

"I, uh, was getting something for Victor. It's a surprise for Amelie, so he hid it, but then I forgot..." I'm babbling. I read a book once, where a woman couldn't lie to the man she loved, and I thought it was the stupidest thing in the world. Love has nothing to do with truth. But this may be the most important lie I've ever told in my life, and my mind's gone blank of everything but the truth.

Seth takes a step toward me. "You're helping Victor?"

"No! No, I'm helping Amelie. Barbie orchestrated it. It's a kind of thank you—"

"Why didn't you tell me?" he asks, confused.

"Slipped my mind. Then you were asleep, and I…" The words go dry in my mouth as Seth reaches for the canvas.

My fingers tighten instinctively. *No. No, no, no, no.*

Seth waits. I can feel the waves of suspicion radiating off him in the dark.

I force my fingers to let go.

This isn't the only time he's held one of my forgeries, I tell myself. That first day, on the sidewalk, he picked up my forged painting, and he handed it back because Seth doesn't take what's not his.

I say it like a mantra in my head as his fingers take in the weight of the painting. The texture of a two-hundred-plus-year-old canvas.

I can tell the moment he realizes it's special because he hits a light switch, and the whole hallway lights up like Christmas Day.

I flinch. There's nowhere to hide.

Seth looks down at the painting in his hands. "Jesus bloody Christ."

His face is awed as he takes it in. The woods, the figures, the colors. The signature.

"Is it real?" he asks without looking up.

I don't say anything, which seems to answer his question.

Seth looks up, and he isn't confused anymore. He's hurt. "This is a new Vivian LaBlanc. And you're giving it to *Victor*."

He has no idea how new. "I'm not *giving* it to him. It's his painting. I helped him hide it—"

"But you *helped*. Why would you…" He frowns.

His expression clears with sudden, angry understanding, and I feel my pulse speed up.

"This isn't a thank you. It's a tactic. He's trying to win the inheritance. And you're working with him."

"Seth, it's not like that—"

"After what I told you." His hands clench the canvas frame so hard, I worry it will snap. "I know you don't care about me like I do about you. But don't you care at all?"

"Of course I care." My voice is a wreck, cracking and shaking.

"Then why are you helping him?" Seth roars. "He betrayed me, Darcy. He fucking— Why would you help him?"

He searches my face, desperate for a reason to still believe in me. "Does he have something on you?"

Fear flashes through me. He's getting too close.

I back away, shaking my head. "Stop, Seth. Please stop."

He tosses the "priceless" painting on a side table and carefully reaches for me. "Help me understand, Darcy."

"You said you trusted me." My back hits the wall, and I run out of ways to get away from this man I can't lie to. Seth lifts his hand to caress my cheek, and I flinch.

The hurt and confusion that flares in his eyes is banked so fast I almost don't see it. But that's the moment everything changes.

Seth drops his hand. "It looks like you're the one who doesn't trust *me*."

His voice is hollow, and he looks forlorn, standing there in the hallway, the angles of his body sharp, his hair a mess.

He's wearing the pajamas I bought him. Something about that detail breaks my heart.

The truth rises up in my mouth like bile.

Look down at the signature. See the echo. I got the idea from the way you signed all those pages. Look down, and realize I'm not trying to betray you.

But I can't tell Seth I'm a criminal. I can't.

Maybe if we'd just met. Maybe if I believed in fairy tales and happy endings and a world where good things happened.

But I've known him for two years and three months, and I know: that would be one lie too many. One thing he couldn't forgive.

Seth looks back at the painting, numb. "Is this a forgery? Is he...again?"

He faces me, and it's like I can see him retreating into his take-care-of-others mode, because that's easier to focus on than how I'm hurting him. "If it's a forgery, Victor *can't* give it to Amelie. If she insured it or donated it... I'm getting this verified. Then if it's real I'll give it back to Victor."

"No." He's terrifying me. He can't get it verified. "It's real."

"How do you know?"

"Because I found it."

As soon as the words are out of my mouth, I know they're a mistake.

He tenses, his color high. "You found it. And you're giving it to Victor. This has nothing to do with Barbie. You found a painting *you knew* could tilt Amelie's opinion, and you're giving it to Victor."

I've never seen him this furious, but I can't argue. I've built a house of cards, and if I correct him about one lie, the whole thing comes crashing down.

"It's not what you think," I say helplessly. I grab his face, trying to break through his anger. "Trust me. I swear it's the last thing I'll ever ask you to take on faith."

Our eyes meet. I hold my breath. Then he turns and walks away.

"Wait."

He doesn't.

"Seth, I'd do anything for you. You know that right?" My face is wet. I'm crying.

Seth turns back, and his eyes are bright too. "I want this one thing. For you not to give the painting to my brother."

I close my eyes. "I can't do that."

"Why?"

I turn around and slam my fist into the wall, so hard the real, non-forged paintings shake.

But I don't tell him why. Neither of us moves. The clock chimes four-thirty in the morning. The sun will be up in a matter of hours.

Seth takes a deep, ragged breath. I hear him take a step, and for a heartbeat, I think he's coming to me. To take me in his arms. To figure this out.

But he's walking away. *He's walking away.*

I whirl. "We're not the kind of people who walk away. That's what you said that time in the office. You said we stay, and we fix this."

He rounds on me. "We, Darcy, *we*. I can't fix it if you won't stop or listen, or at least tell me *why*." His fist is balled, tense, like he wants to hit something, but as always, Seth's better controlled than me. He glares, his chest heaving like he's run a mile.

And then his shoulders slump. He looks away.

Now I know true, awful panic. *Seth's giving up.* He's giving up on me, on us. It's in every line of his body.

"There's no coming back from this, is there?" I ask. "If I give this to Victor."

"Not if you can't tell me why." His voice is so weary it breaks my heart.

I can't tell him why. And I can't lose him.

Which leaves one option. My hands shake as I pick up the painting.

"Here. It's yours," I press it into his reluctant hands.

"But why were you going to—"

"No." I shake my head. "You can't ask me that. I'm giving you the painting. But you can't ask me why ever again." I search his clear blue eyes. "Can you live with that?"

Seth lifts his hand toward me. Then hesitates, like he's remembering me flinching.

I take his hand and press it against my cheek, leaning into his touch. Something in him begins to uncoil.

"Yeah," he says, his voice rough. "I can live with that."

His eyes are still haunted, but he kisses me once, fierce, like he's trying to rescue us both.

Seth pulls back before I'm ready.

But I'm scared he'll pull back even farther if I ask for more.

***

Downstairs, we get in bed without touching each other or speaking.

Half of me is in the thick of this pain with Seth, trying to figure out how to repair this fragile, nearly broken bridge between us.

The other half is making a to-do list. *Cancel the reporters. Paint over the mirrored signature. Destroy the painting before Amelie tries to get it insured. Arson? Figure out what to tell Victor. A dozen forgeries over the next few years in exchange for his silence?*

I roll over to face Seth as the cold, cruel gray of pre-dawn seeps into the room.

How many crimes would I commit to keep this man?

A lifetime of them.

Somehow I don't think Seth would find that an admirable trait. As if he senses my eyes on him, Seth shifts to face me. His face is pure and hurt and tired and good and beautiful, and my throat tightens against the tears.

Seth reaches out across the vast expanse of the bed and takes my hand.

"It's ok. You can go to sleep now. We're going to be ok," he says. In his hushed, deep voice it sounds like a promise. "We're not the kind of people who walk away."

I close my eyes to keep from tearing up and hang on to his promise like a raft in a storm. When the panic rises, because how am I going to solve all of this, I focus on that promise, and breathe, and breathe, and breathe.

I'm so tired.

As soon as Seth falls asleep, I'll get up and cancel the reporters, paint over the name. As soon as he falls asleep.

I lie still and listen to his breathing. Hold his hand in mine. Let his presence sink into me, calm me…

When my eyes fly open, it's morning. Seth and the painting are gone.

Chapter Seventeen

Seth

When I arrive in the breakfast room with the painting in hand, Victor is standing across from Barbie, his jaw tensed in the stubborn way it gets when he knows he's in the wrong. Barbie's leaning across the table, about to say something, when she sees me, and her mouth snaps shut.

Amelie's not here yet. *Good.*

Barbie looks at the painting, and her eyes widen. She knows this is important, and that's viciously satisfying. She knows this damn thing can fuck up lives.

"Barbie, will you excuse us?" I ask, my voice clipped.

"Oh don't mind me, I'll sit here and drink my coffee—"

"*Now*," I say, and I'm surprised to realize I sound like my father.

Barbie rises, expressionless, her eyes sweeping the room as she leaves like she's taking mental pictures of everything. As soon as the door closes, I turn to Victor. We size each other up over the table. I've been avoiding this moment since he betrayed me. What good would it do?

But he's fucking with me through Darcy. So this stops now.

I slam the painting onto the breakfast table, dangerously close to the jam, and Victor winces.

"Where did you get it?" he asks warily.

"You know where I got it," I spit. "What the hell do you have on her?"

Victor smirks. "What makes you think I have something on her? Maybe she likes me better than you."

I snarl, but he laughs.

"When will you ever learn, baby brother? You can't get something for nothing," he taunts. His eyes drop to the painting. "Luckily for you, you have something I want."

My fingers tighten on the canvas. God, I hate him. I've kept his secret for two fucking years, and this is how he repays me.

"You know what? I'm done." I take the painting off the table.

He snorts. "Done with what? Whining? Being a bloody pushover?"

"Done keeping your secret," I lie.

The blood drains from Victor's face, making him look eerily gothic in his black velvet. *My brother the vampire.*

"What secret?" Victor shrugs, but the motion is jerky.

"That you tried to send me to a site raided by the FBI, filled with forged paintings. I know for a fact one of the paintings they collected was previously in your possession, and you knew it was a forgery. I have a well-respected insurance fraud investigator who can corroborate both of those last two details."

Victor jerks back like he's been slapped. "You wouldn't... That doesn't mean anything... They'd send me to prison. American prison."

I slam my hand on the table. "You tried to do the same thing to me,"

"It wouldn't have stuck. You were clean as a whistle, a bloody boy scout."

"But why did it have to be *me*?" I say. I'm ashamed that my voice breaks. But there it is. The shameful truth. I'm not furious that my brother is a selfish, unforgivable dick. He's been that his whole life.

I'm furious he did it to *me*.

"So this is what it's all about," Victor says, his voice quiet. "Revenge. You've been holding on to your anger for years. And now you're going to cash in and send me to jail because you can't stand the fact Darcy picked me over you."

"No. I would have kept your secret to the grave," I say.

"Then why—"

"Because you threatened Darcy."

"You love her more than you love me," Victor says, stunned.

It should be funny because of course I fucking love her more than Victor. For starters, she never set up an elaborate plan to throw me to the FBI. Instead, it's bleakly tragic. Love isn't supposed to be a ranking system.

Victor's the one who turned it into one.

He seems to catch my hesitation. "You wouldn't tell," he says, his shoulders straightening. "You're bluffing."

Imagine the whole story in your head, I hear Darcy say in my mind. *They'll see the things you're not saying.*

So I think of the awful, unmitigated rage I felt last night when Darcy picked Victor over me. I think of grabbing him in the library, the first night when he scared her. I think of what I'd want to do if she left me.

Worse, what I'd *actually* do if someone hurt her.

"You don't get it. You've never protected anything but yourself," I say quietly. "But I'm not you. And I will protect her, at any cost."

"Even me?" he tries to snarl, but there's fear in his eyes, and it's about damn time, but it's horrible too. My brother is afraid of me.

"Yes, Victor," I lie. "Even you."

The fight goes out of him. He grips the back of a chair for support, his head down. He looks smaller now. I'm a bit taller, but he's always been broader, tougher, stronger. For the first time, those two inches feel like a foot.

"You're going to tell me why and how you threatened her," I say, in an authoritative voice which sounds like our father again. "And then you're *never* going to come after her again, or I go straight to the cops. Got it?"

"Yes, fine, 'got it.'" Victor looks up at me, and for the first time, there's a flicker of sympathy on his face. He looks like the older brother I miss. "But are you sure you want to know what I blackmailed her with?"

Darcy's face from last night flashes in front of me: wild-eyed, exhausted, weary, scared. *You can't ask me that. You can't ask me why ever again.*

The ground feels like it's sinking under me. For the first time this morning, I feel afraid. There's nothing Darcy could have done that would change how I feel. That would change us. Right? Suddenly it feels like a betrayal to drag it out of Victor before Darcy's willing to tell me herself.

At least that's what I tell myself as I scramble for solid ground, tucking the painting under my arm. "Fine. But I'm taking the painting with me."

"The hell you are It's a Vivian LaBlanc. You don't even like impressionists."

"I like this one," I say, heading toward the door.

"Figures," he says under his breath, but there's something about the way he says it that makes the hairs on the back of my neck stand up.

"What do you mean?" I say, slowly turning back to face him.

Victor smirks. "Seems you have remarkably consistent taste."

"Boys, we have company. The wedding reporter is here, and she's brought a photographer…" Amelie beams as she strides into the room, followed by two middle-aged white women I don't know, one dressed in loose gray and beige and holding an audio recorder, the other smartly dressed with an artsy scarf and a camera.

The reporter smiles at us blandly, until her eyes catch the painting. Her jaw drops. "*Merde*. She was telling the truth."

The photographer lets go of her camera so abruptly it swings from the strap around her neck. She whips on a pair of white gloves.

"May I?" she asks, but she's already stepping toward me, her hands outstretched.

"Seth, what's going on?" Amelie asks, confused.

"Seth, is that your painting?" Barbie asks from over Amelie's shoulder. She looks at me meaningfully. "Because if it's not, now would be a great time to mention it."

"It's mine," I say defensively, as Darcy skids into view behind Amelie and Barbie. She's wild-haired, and still in her pajama shorts, with the thin, drapey pink t-shirt with the gold lettering on it.

"I'd like to examine it," the photographer says like it's her right to. She sounds less like a photographer, and more like the people I know who handle art professionally.

"If that's a real LaBlanc…" she says in hushed, reverent tones.

"It is," I say before I catch Darcy's frantic head shaking. *What the hell?*

"Wonderful." The photographer plucks the painting out of my hands.

Darcy looks like she's going to throw up. The photographer slowly examines the painting, poring over the work with a portable light underneath a magnifying glass. She flips the canvas over, checking the back. Her thumb hovers over a little imperfection, where the wooden frame has been slightly warped by the tension of the canvas.

"Well?" the reporter demands, seeming way too eager for a wedding reporter.

Something's going on. I look at Darcy questioningly, but her face is alarmingly blank.

My stomach twists. *She knows what's going on.*

The photographer who's not a photographer surveys the painting. "I'd have to do some tests, and get a second, and third opinion, before anyone loaned it to a museum. But at first glance, the age of the canvas, the color choice, the brushstrokes..." She frowns. "It *feels* like a LaBlanc. It feels...trapped and free at the same time."

Behind everyone, Darcy sags against the doorframe. She closes her eyes, and I can't tell if it's from relief or something else. When she opens her eyes and sees me watching her, something fierce takes over her expression.

My pulse is pounding. I want to grab her and demand she tell me what's going on, but there are all these people around.

Including my aunt, who's looking at the LaBlanc with something akin to worship.

Maybe Victor had the right idea about one thing.

I clear my throat. "Amelie, if you want—"

"*C'est un faux,*" the photographer yells, like she's been personally betrayed. She jabs a finger at the pond. "The signature. Vivian never signed her paintings with her *own* name. And even if she had, that's not her signature."

I look at Darcy, confused. "You said..." I can't finish the sentence. *She wouldn't lie to me.* She wouldn't let me walk off with a forgery. Not when my entire professional reputation depends on people trusting my word and my instincts.

Not when my life's savings is sitting in an escrow account, waiting to be transferred to her at the drop of a wedding photograph.

A photograph that would be pretty damn easy to photoshop.

No. Don't go there. You're spiraling. It's Darcy. You trust her. You love her.

The reporter turns the voice recorder to me. "Mr. Moreau. You tried to pass off a forgery to the press. What do you have to say for yourself?"

I shake my head, trying to get a grip.

"Did you think you could take advantage of your aunt's standing in the community to hoodwink a local paper into giving your ridiculous claim the publicity a national paper wouldn't?" the reporter demands.

"Stop it, just stop," Darcy cries.

"Why were you rushing a wedding that was, by all accounts, unplanned when you stepped on French soil?" the reporter presses.

"Enough," Amelie barks. "The wedding was my idea."

"Was the painting your idea too?" the reporter asks Amelie, and as Amelie hesitates, I can see the pieces falling horribly into place.

If Amelie doesn't disavow the painting, and thus me, she'll lose the respect of her community. The people she spends her life with the ninety percent of the year when none of her family is here.

All because I lied and said I had a fiancée.

"No," I say. "The painting is mine. I was told it was authentic. Obviously, I had plans to get it authenticated—"

"Then why did your fiancée invite us to come to breakfast today to see Mr. Moreau unveil a never-before-seen masterpiece?" the reporter asks.

I feel like I've been punched. Darcy didn't... Darcy wouldn't...

But that's what I thought about Victor. And he was my *brother*.

You'd think after what I did to you, you'd be less of a goddamn mark. But you'll believe anything she fucking says.

"Are the other paintings you sell forged?" the reporter asks.

My ears are ringing.

"Mr. Moreau. Do you have anything to say for yourself?"

I try to focus on the reporter—on the recorder being jammed into my face. "I was told it was real," I say in a daze.

"Told by whom?" the reporter demands, and it's everything I can do not to look at Darcy.

She's screwing me over, and I still can't stop myself from trying to protect her.

"The ladies bring up an excellent point," Barbie drawls. "Who told you it was real, Seth?"

I shut my mouth mulishly.

"Right. If that's how you want to play it," Barbie sighs.

Then she whips out an FBI badge and a pair of cuffs. "Seth Moreau, I'm arresting you for forgery."

There's a moment of stunned silence as everyone stares at Barbie.

All hell breaks loose. The reporter starts yelling questions at Barbie, at the same time as the photographer starts effusively apologizing for contaminating evidence, while Amelie rubs her heart.

One look at Victor's slack jaw tells me he's as shocked as the rest of us, but then he recovers, slipping out a side door as Barbie advances on me, cuffs in hand.

"Please, Barbie, you know me—"

"I thought I did. I *really* didn't expect it to be you." She's snapping the first cuff on my wrist when Darcy's voice cuts through the din.

"It was me. I forged the painting."

All eyes turn to Darcy. Her chin is raised defiantly, her arms crossed over her chest. Confessing to criminal activity barefoot in her pajamas, daring the world to think less of her.

"I forged the painting. I lied to Seth. I told him it was real. He's innocent. So is Amelie."

"How do I know you're not lying to get your lover off the hook?" Barbie asks, with neutral, professional focus. Even the way she stands has changed.

We all lie to each other so easily. The metal of the cuff is cold on my wrist.

Darcy ignores me, focusing on Barbie. "Scrape away the bottom right-hand corner. There's a stain on the canvas. Like the outline of a very poorly drawn pear."

Barbie looks at the photographer. "I'm assuming you're not a photographer."

"Dr. Florand, at your service. Specializing in impressionists, with a focus on Vivian LaBlanc. I care for the archives at the LaBlanc house and museum."

"Right then." Barbie points to the painting. "Scrape."

Dr. Florand hesitates.

"What's the matter?" Barbie asks.

"... It's a really good fake."

"Are you worried you're wrong?" Barbie asks pointedly.

"*Non.* But it's a shame to destroy something this beautiful."

"Oh for God's sake." Darcy grabs a knife off the breakfast table and, before anyone can stop her, kneels next to the painting and starts scraping away. Even before the stained shape on the canvas is revealed, I know she's telling the truth.

Dr. Florand handled the art carefully, like a scholar. Darcy wrestles with it like the woman who gave birth to the damn thing.

When she's done, Darcy sits back on her heels. She looks calm, but I can see the hand clenching the knife is shaking.

For the second time in a matter of minutes, the room is silent as everyone takes in what the centuries-old stain means. Darcy Sherwood is a world-class art forger.

Suddenly the pieces start flying into place. Darcy needing a name change to hide from someone. Victor acting like he knew Darcy. Having something he could blackmail her with. The master forger in the ring, the one they never caught.

Hell, even meeting her blocks away from the FBI raid.

My eyes fly to Darcy's. "How could you?"

She looks away from me to Barbie. "I told you, Seth's innocent. He and Amelie have nothing to do with this."

Barbie purses her lips. "I love a sacrificial romantic gesture as much as the next woman, but because you were the one to paint it doesn't mean—"

"You're not here because you care about this painting. You're here because of the forgery ring two years ago, right?" Darcy demands.

"You got something you want to tell me, honey?" Barbie says.

Darcy rises, dignified. "If you want me to tell you, you have to uncuff him."

Barbie hesitates.

"I said Seth and Amelie are innocent. I didn't say anything about Victor," Darcy says, and I whip my head toward her.

She said she wouldn't tell. She flinches at the fury in my eyes.

"Don't look at me like that," Darcy says as Barbie unlocks the cuff on my hand and snaps it on Darcy. "I get to decide whether or not I tell my secrets. I decide who I save."

I don't know why I'm surprised. It's one more in a long line of betrayals.

Barbie snaps the other cuff on Darcy's wrist, grabs the painting, and walks her out of the room. "Dr. Florand, if I could have a ride to the local police station?"

"I'll take you," the reporter pipes up. As they're walking out of the house, I hear her asking Barbie if she wants to make a statement.

Amelie rushes to the window while I stand there, trying to understand what happened. Amelie watches them drive away, her hand pressed to the glass.

When she turns back to me, her face is filled with compassion. "Don't worry, Seth. We'll get Darcy back. I swear. She wasn't trying to sell the painting, for heaven's sake. And you're not pressing charges. As long as she doesn't say anything incriminating about whatever that forgery ring nonsense was—"

"Don't bother," I say. "She's not my fiancée."

Chapter Eighteen

Darcy

I'll say this for small towns in Burgundy. Even their police stations are quainter than ours. I'm sitting alone in a clean, bare room with faded light blue walls, an old wooden table, and dingy light bulbs. Barbie even took the cuffs back when she shut me in here.

Or maybe it's that Barbie's going easy on me. We were almost fake sisters-in-law, after all.

I laugh because Barbie is fucking FBI, but I sound broken, like a wounded animal.

I press my forehead to the table and try to breathe. I can't believe how wrong this went. The look on Seth's face, when he thought someone he loved had set him up again...

It makes me want to cry, and shout, and comfort him. Swear I'll never do that. I'd do a lot of things, but never that.

Except I accidentally did. And I don't think it's something Seth can forgive.

I choke back a sob. Half of it is the rising grief of losing him. But half of it is the fact I'm alone in a French police station because Barbie has a contact.

And the only people who know I'm here—hell, the only people in France who know me—hate me.

I groan and scrub my face. I didn't know it was possible to be so alone. Maybe James will think to look for me when I don't show up for our divorce next month.

I make myself sit up, breathe deeply. Any moment Barbie's going to come back. I have to figure out some way to convince

Barbie to give me immunity in exchange for testifying against Victor.

Otherwise, I'm going to jail.

Although to be honest, right this second, that seems like a thing that might as well happen. It would match the rest of the day.

I flash to our hotel room in Paris, Seth smiling lazily up at me from the pillows in the early morning light. It's the happiest I can remember ever being, as an adult.

I'd been more than happy really. Happiness is clear, fresh morning light. This had depth to it. Like the thick golden glow before the sun sets. Like joy.

Like love. Fuck, I love him. I love him so much, I could howl with it.

What's that Shakespeare line? "My only love, sprung from my only hate"?

I always hated tragedies.

The doorknob clicks, and I snap to alertness as Barbie walks into the room, carrying two cups of coffee. She sits down across the table and slides the coffee to me.

I haven't had any coffee yet today—I haven't had breakfast, now I think about it—and the hot, strong scent wakes up every craving I have.

I cross my arms and lean back in my chair. "I'm not falling for that. You're not getting my DNA without a warrant."

Barbie rolls her eyes. "We've been living together for almost a month. If I wanted your DNA, I'd have it."

She...brings up a good point.

My stomach growls.

"You know, caffeine is an appetite suppressant," Barbie says. "And I'm sure as hell not feeding you any time soon."

"I'll try to plan for that the next time I get arrested," I say, and Barbie bursts out laughing.

It's not the giggle she's been doing all month. It's big and hearty and throaty, not unlike a big-hearted grandma with a pack-a-day habit.

It doesn't make me feel better. It does make me trust her more. I have no doubt she'll take me down, but she's not going to lie to me while she does it.

I think of her warning, that day when I was looking up art forgery busts at Amelie's. Barbie could have easily entrapped me into doing something incriminating. Instead, she all but warned me off. Even today, I could have avoided getting caught if I'd been willing to leave Seth hanging.

I take the coffee. The heat and kick hits me like a welcome jolt of electricity, shoving me in the direction of normalcy.

My gut says Barbie's after much bigger fish than me. All I need to do is help her catch that fish. I'm about to verbally vomit everything I know about Victor and the forgery ring, and hope for the best, when I hear Seth's words from a million business negotiations in my head: *Never bargain against yourself.*

"So," I say, taking another sip of my coffee. "What would I have to give you on Victor to get immunity?"

"You think you can get immunity from being a ringleader in the biggest forgery ring in the last decade because you can tell us Victor is dirty and water is wet?" Barbie drawls, her face impassive.

My stomach tightens, but I keep my face bland, like Seth would. *Just another negotiation. And you learned from the best.*

I put my elbows on the table and prop my chin on my laced fingers like this conversation is no more important than deciding where we should go for lunch.

"I think you have no way of connecting me to the forgery ring," I say. "I think the master forger you're hunting for hasn't put out a painting in two years, as far as you know. So either they've gotten so good you'll never catch them, or they've reformed, and it will be pretty anticlimactic if you expose them. Some people might not even believe you."

"I think," Barbie says, mimicking my posture, "they did a painting this week. A painting we have in our custody. I'm thinking when we compare it to a certain Monet we have in the evidence locker…"

I force myself to stay calm. I hadn't thought of that.

"Even if that works," I make myself say, "it only gives you the forger. Not the ringleader. So I'm asking. If I could give you Victor Moreau, if you could have your ringleader…would you give me immunity for anything I may or may not have done?"

Barbie leans back and drums her bubblegum-pink nails on the table. Like she's deciding whether I'm full of shit.

She's deciding how much to risk, I hear Seth correct me in my head.

Which, you know, *rude*.

But imaginary Seth is right. I need to tempt Barbie's ambition. I need to make the risk irresistible. If I can't, there's a good chance I'm spending the foreseeable future in jail.

I sip my coffee and study her the way she's studying me. Trying to see what I'm missing.

"How long have you been undercover?" I ask.

The question startles her. "That's not relevant."

"Because you blew months' worth of work to stop someone from giving a painting to his aunt. They hadn't even tried to insure it yet. If your experts can't connect my forgery to whatever painting you have on file, you don't even have your forger. And Victor's guard will be up after this. The FBI's not going to get an undercover agent this close again."

Barbie tilts her chin up. "You don't know what you're talking about."

I lean over the table. "Maybe not. But I know you. You're the kind of woman who gets her mark. And I'm telling you, he's in your sights. All you have to do is let me help."

"I'm not stopping you."

"Cut the shit, Barbie. Neither of us are idiots, despite what Victor thought."

She shifts, rage flashing in her eyes.

Good, I hit a nerve.

I spread my hands. "So tell me. What do I have to give you to get immunity?"

Her eyes narrow. "You don't get immunity from anything violent."

I nod. "I didn't do violence."

"Then I'd need evidence. And testimony. The other forgers we caught won't talk."

I think of the group I met. None of us were loyal to Victor. But if they were going down no matter what... "He's paying them off," I say.

Barbie shrugs noncommittally, but I can tell she agrees with me. "We're monitoring his bank account and theirs. So far nothing's moved on either end."

"He doesn't pay with money. I mean. Hypothetically," I say. Barbie rolls her eyes and motions for me to continue.

I bite my lip. I shouldn't say more. Not without some kind of official agreement.

But it's not like I can afford the kind of lawyer who could get me out of this. Which means I need to try to stay in Barbie's good graces and help her catch Victor.

"He doesn't pay cash after the first few jobs," I say. "Once he's got a forger hooked, he pays with an item of great value. A diamond. An antique. A stock tip. Normally it's something he shouldn't have. It's up to the forger to figure out how to convert it into money. People with an appetite for risk could make thousands for a few hours' work."

She raises her eyebrow. "And the forgers without an appetite for risk?"

"Hypothetically, I'd say they got ripped off at a lot of pawnshops because having things like that in their possession made their skin itch."

"Hypothetically, I'd say instinct probably helped them avoid getting caught," Barbie says, and we share wry, wary smiles over our coffee. Barbie sighs. "I won't lie, that's helpful. But I need more than that." She rises and turns to go.

"I can testify he hired me," I say, standing. "I can tell you which paintings he commissioned, and when. I can describe everyone in the organization I met. Give you everyone's code names."

Barbie turns back to me. "All of that's helpful, but none of it's proof. I'd be putting a broke forger with a history of lying on the stand against one of the most powerful, charming men in the New York art world. Think, Darcy. I need you to give me the knife that will take him down."

I brace myself on the table, staring blankly down at the scarred wood as I rack my brains. Victor was always so careful to keep things separate. I never even knew where he lived, although I assumed it was somewhere around the Astoria, Queens neighborhood because the only time he was ever late for meetings was when the Q and N trains were fucked up.

I blink. Seth mentioned his brother lived in some grand historic place on the Upper East Side he couldn't afford. That was before I realized his brother was V., obviously, so I didn't think anything of it.

If Victor didn't live out there…

He only seemed to come from that direction when he had a payment to give me. "Wherever he stores the things he pays people with. It's somewhere in Astoria. I think."

Something in Barbie's face falls. "That's it? All you can tell me?"

My stomach sinks. "It's not enough, is it?"

She gives me a hard look and leaves. I slump down into my chair. I'm screwed. I am so, so screwed.

I'm going to have to get over a broken heart in jail where there's no ice cream.

The door clicks open, and I jump.

Barbie throws down a notebook and pencil in front of me. "Tell me everything you remember about every time you met. Where, when, the assignment, the payment. Everything."

"I don't want to incriminate myself if it wouldn't be enough to get immunity," I argue, but the fight's gone out of me. Their art expert will catch me, and I don't have anything else to barter with.

Barbie grabs the pencil and writes HYPOTHETICALLY in big bold letters across the top of the page then shoves the notebook at me. "Fine then. Give me hypotheticals."

I snort. "Hypotheticals you can then use to find evidence on security cameras—"

"Evidence I can use to convict him," Barbie says. "Trust me on this, Sherwood. I am damn good at my job."

I take the pencil, still making up my mind.

She starts to leave.

"Where are you going?" I ask.

"To talk to Seth and Amelie. You narrowed it down to Astoria. Let's see if they can narrow it down further."

I shake my head. "They wouldn't know. They're as clean as they come. And even if they did, they wouldn't betray family."

"Yeah, that was before they fell in love with you," Barbie says.

She disappears behind a locked door before I can explain to her how very wrong she is about that. No one's in love with me. Not the whole me.

If Amelie won't pick Seth over Victor, she's certainly not going to pick *me* over Victor.

And Seth, well… I swipe at my tears.

I'm going to have to save myself on this one. Face the consequences and throw everything I can into taking Victor Moreau down. I couldn't do it by myself. But with Barbie's help, maybe I can.

I use the paint-flecked elastic on my wrist to scoop my hair into a messy bun. I grab my coffee.

Then I start writing.

Chapter Nineteen

Seth

I'm standing in our room, staring at Darcy's red velvet ankle boots lined up by her suitcase.

I feel like someone pulled the rug out from under the last two years of my life. This whole time I've been trusting a criminal with my business—with million-dollar artwork, with checks, with private information about the richest art collectors in New York.

Worse, a criminal who worked with Victor.

I think of Darcy in Monet's garden, convinced she wasn't good enough to paint it. I thought it was artistic insecurity, but now I know what it was: guilt.

God, how much else did I miss?

The Vivian LaBlanc book I got her lies on her bedside table, taunting me. She probably used it for her forgery.

I hurl the book across the room. It slams into the wall, chipping plaster, as Amelie opens the door. She looks at the book on the floor, then the nick in the wall, with disbelief. Probably not something she expects from the *good* brother.

"I'd ask you to pay for that," Amelie says in a damn sorry attempt at a joke, "but it will be yours someday anyway."

"No. It will be Victor's." I don't realize I've made up my mind until the words are out of my mouth, but once they're out, I'm certain. There's been too much lying, and I'm fucking *done*.

I grab my shirts out of the closet, yanking them out from between the rainbow of Darcy's dresses, and start packing.

"Seth? What are you doing?" Amelie asks, alarmed.

"I shouldn't have lied to you about being engaged. The fact Darcy suggested it should have been a clue right there, but I wanted to win. I wanted to beat Victor. I wanted to take care of the family legacy. I wanted you to be proud of me."

"Of course I'm proud of you—"

"Let me finish, Amelie!"

The shock on her face finally breaks through my rage. I take a deep breath. I shouldn't be yelling at Amelie. It's not her fault Darcy's someone I shouldn't have trusted, let alone loved.

Hell, I'm not even sure it's Darcy's fault. Who gives a job to someone they bump into on the sidewalk? Someone who's begging to be conned, that's who.

None of it erases the fact Amelie and I need to talk.

"I'm sorry I shouted. And I'm sorry I lied to you," I say. "But you shouldn't have asked me to produce a fiancée because you felt like having a wedding."

Amelie sits on the settee, looking very tired. "That wasn't what I was trying to do."

"Then what? Did you *want* to see Victor and me duke it out?"

"I was trying to get you to go out on a date. Any date at all. You'd say you wanted to have a family, get married someday. But whenever I asked you what you did this week, it was always work. You even stopped going out with your friends. I wanted you to prioritize your personal life, for once. I knew the only way to get you to do that was if I gave you a deadline and a good kick in the arse."

I sit down on the bed, stunned.

"I never expected you to pull it off. Either of you. You're too careful, and Victor is… well, a work in progress. I kept expecting you or Darcy to crack, or Barbie to lose her temper and confess. Then we could all laugh, and you could relax and enjoy the first real vacation you've had in *years* with the assistant you were obviously in love with."

"No. You're wrong about that." I stand, and go back to packing, kneeling in front of my suitcase to shove stuff in with unnecessary viciousness. "I fell in love with her because of lies. She even tried to tell me it wasn't real, but I wouldn't listen."

"Hogwash. I knew you were in love with her the instant I saw the two of you on FaceTime. You've always lived for your work, but these last few years…" Amelie shrugs a delicate shoulder. "You couldn't ask her out. And you couldn't give her up. So instead you lied to yourself and spent as much time as you could working next to her."

I snort. "That's some revisionist history."

"Seth. Look at me."

I pivot on my knees away from the suitcase. Amelie's leaning forward on the settee, her hands braced on her knees, her eyes bright.

"You have loved her for years and will continue loving her for years. I know love, and I know you. Your love is unconditional."

I stand, my hands shaking with the need to make her understand. "Unconditional is dangerous, Amelie. She betrayed me, like Victor, and I can't..." My voice cracks. "I can't keep giving everything I have to people who are going to destroy me."

"Oh, my dear boy." She rises, crosses the room, and reaches up to cup my face. She used to do that when I skinned my knee, and she was going to impart some great wisdom. Except then I was the one looking up at her.

I can see her eyes glistening.

"She didn't betray you," Amelie says. "She spoke up. She took your place. She proved irrevocably she did it, and you were innocent. She didn't betray you. She gave herself up to save you."

I briefly close my eyes and step back, shaking my head, because I want so badly to believe her. It's a physical ache, wanting to believe in Darcy.

"But what about the reporters?" I ask. "She called the reporters and said Mr. Moreau had a painting. Even if she wasn't trying to send me to jail, she was trying to use me—"

Amelie puts her hands on her hips. "When did you get the painting? Because I talked to the reporters, and she called them yesterday. And there's more than one Mr. Moreau on the premises. Although I can't see why she'd want to use Victor. Or how she could have known her fake would be caught..."

Amelie keeps working through possibilities, but I stop listening as my eyes fall on the Vivian LeBlanc book by the wall.

The one where I signed the correct name on every page for her.

The thing that tipped off the expert was the signature.

Darcy *knew* what the signature should have been. But Victor probably wouldn't have looked closely. After all, Darcy had never been caught before.

Victor blackmailed her into doing the painting for him. But she figured out a way for him to be caught before he benefited from it. If I'd only let her give him the painting…

But I ruined it because I couldn't trust her. Now she's off in handcuffs paying the price.

Oh God. I need to go save her. I need—

I pace to the window, running my hands through my hair. Darcy still lied to me for *years*.

And maybe I get that when we were employer and employee. But here, in France… She could have said something any number of times. When she recognized Victor at the airport. When she told me she was married. In the car when I told her about Victor framing me.

I look out at the gray sky.

"She's a criminal," I say, but I can hear the uncertainty in my voice.

"Did she ever steal from you, in all the years you trusted her?" she asks.

No. Never.

"Why didn't she tell me?" I wheel to face Amelie. "I could have protected her if she'd only *told* me."

Amelie smiles quietly. "Why does anyone keep secrets? Fear."

It's a woefully inadequate answer.

But it's the best answer I'm going to get if I don't go talk to Darcy.

Fuck, I don't even know where she's locked up.

I'm deep in my head, coming up with a million off-the-wall plans to free Darcy, when Amelie puts her hands on my shoulders.

"In any event, here's one last secret. You're inheriting the chateau and everything in it. It's been in the will for the last ten years."

I blink. "But… that was before he—"

She pats me on the cheek. "It's not about Victor. It's about you. And you've been the right person to choose how to carry this family's legacy since before you could drink. The will formalizes it."

"I… I don't know what to say."

"You don't have to say, or do, anything. It's…a kind of unconditional trust." She clears her throat. "I do love you, my dear boy."

I swallow, my throat suddenly tight. "I—"

"I know," Amelie cuts me off, clearly uncomfortable with the amount of sincerity we've displayed. She waves a dismissive hand at me as she heads to the door. "Go figure out how to save your princess."

***

I'm on my laptop frantically trying to get a hold of a lawyer specializing in international art fraud when my cell phone rings. It's an unknown number, and I almost don't answer it, but at the last second, I realize it might be Darcy.

I grab the phone. "Hello? Darcy?"

"Barbie," a Southern-tinged voice says. "Sorry to disappoint."

"What have you done with her? Where is she? Is she ok?" Visions of Darcy in a dark cell flash through my mind.

"Calm down. She's warm and caffeinated and half the station is in love with her. I anticipate a lovely lunch spread in her future."

I sink back into the couch with relief. "Can I talk to her?"

"No. But I can do you one better. You can talk to me," Barbie says.

"How is that better?" I bite out. "You lied to all of us. You brought a gun into my aunt's house and told me it was a sex toy."

"In fairness to me, if you had a better knowledge of sex toys, that probably wouldn't have worked. And it's better," she says over my protests, "because if you give me proof Victor was the ringleader of the forgery ring five years ago, Darcy goes free. We're on the clock. Victor left France and may very well be going to destroy evidence."

I freeze. I was bluffing this morning when I told Victor I'd turn him in for Darcy.

Now Barbie's making it a real choice.

"She's going to go free anyway," I say. "I'm hiring the best lawyer in this goddamn country."

"With what money? Your entire savings is in an escrow account. An account, I might add, that doesn't make you or Miss Sherwood look particularly innocent," Barbie says.

"How do you—"

"We've been watching everyone related to Victor. He's the one we want, not Darcy. If you can give me some proof—"

"Let me talk to her," I say, my heart pounding. I need Darcy to tell me the whole truth before I betray my brother.

I know how much betrayal hurts. At least Victor could tell himself I'd get off. If I betray him, he's going down for it. Who knows how long he'd stay locked up?

But if I don't, Darcy pays the cost, and that's unthinkable.

Barbie continues, "Darcy thinks he has a stash house in Astoria, where he keeps stolen goods. If you tell me where it is, and if it's got the evidence we need, I can get Darcy off."

Fuck.

I don't know what the hell she's talking about. If Victor had a stash house, I assumed it was the office that got raided.

"Seth—"

"I don't know." I start pacing. "I don't know."

There's silence on the other end of the line.

Then Barbie sighs heavily. "Fine. One minute. *One.*"

I have no idea what she's talking about, until the background noise increases, then falls away, and I hear Darcy say, "Seth?"

"Darcy, are you ok—"

"I'm fine, I'm so sorry, Seth, and we can talk about everything later, I promise, but I need your help. I'm um," her voice cracks, and it makes me want to break the whole world. "I'm out of rope here. I need you to think where in Astoria Victor would hide something precious."

"Darcy, there's nothing, I already told Barbie, I haven't even been out there since…"

My voice trails off.

I haven't been there since I lived out there, in a tiny, shitty apartment I had when I first moved to the city. An apartment I sublet from Victor.

He said he'd let the lease lapse, but…

It would be the perfect place. Enough families and elderly people in the neighborhood to throw cops and other criminals off the scent. Enough students with high turnover to keep the families and elderly people from noticing one more strange man.

It's there. It has to be. If it's not, I don't know how to save Darcy.

Barbie's right about that much. Until the date for our "wedding" passes without a photo to mark the occasion, my money's tied up.

"Seth, what is it?" Darcy asks. "If you've thought of something, tell me so I can tell Barbie, and she can give me immunity–"

"Have you signed anything?" I interrupt. "Have you signed legal papers saying you get immunity?"

"No, but—"

Barbie takes the phone back. "Tell me what you know, Moreau."

"You haven't given her legal immunity yet."

"You haven't given me *evidence* yet." There's the sound of a door closing, and Barbie's voice lowers. "Come on, Seth, you're not like Victor. Or bless their hearts, Darcy and Amelie. You know there are no shortcuts. Tell me the truth, like you're supposed to. Then I'll place a call, they'll raid the place, and all charges against Darcy will get dismissed. The system will work like it's supposed to."

It's tempting to dump all this in someone else's lap. Barbie's an expert. I'm out of my depth. I can still say I haven't done anything wrong if I tell her.

If I do what I'm thinking… well, that's not something I can say any more. At least not in the eyes of the law. Certainly not in the eyes of my family.

I hesitate. Then I hear Darcy in my head. *She's trying to manipulate you.*

Imaginary Darcy is right. My first duty isn't to the FBI. And it's not to my ass of a brother, or the heartbreak it will cause my parents when I do what I'm about to do.

"If the system worked like it was supposed to, you'd have him already, instead of her," I say, and hang up.

I take out the sim card in my phone so they can't track me and go ask Amelie if she knows anyone whose credit card I can borrow so I can book the first ticket to New York.

Chapter Twenty

Darcy

"Darcy, wake up. Someone's here to see you."

I sit up and blink at Barbie through the bars. I spent the night on a bench in a stall that, as far as I can tell, is mostly used for holding drunks until they sober up. Every muscle is cold and stiff, but the blanket an officer gave me is clean, and no one was drunk or disorderly last night, so I did sleep.

Sort of.

Then what she said catches up with me.

Someone is here to see me.

Seth. It has to be Seth. My heart leaps. I scramble to my feet as Barbie opens the stall door.

"You can see them," she says. "But then we're going to the airport and you and I are going home."

I nod mutely. I spent the whole day yesterday writing down everything I know about Victor. Barbie would come in, flip through pages, then confirm a detail, dial a number on her phone, and leave the room.

I kept waiting for her to come back and tell me a lead had panned out, I'd earned my immunity. But every time she came in, her face was stern, unreadable. Add in Seth's cryptic non-answer, and my hope slowly faded throughout the day.

I step out into the hallway, my heart pounding a racing beat: *I knew he'd come, I knew he'd come, I knew he'd come.*

People like us don't leave.

I follow Barbie out toward the small, sparse waiting room, so certain I'll see him, it feels like fate.

When we enter the waiting room, Seth's not there. My heart sinks.

I made the man who doesn't leave desert me. I broke us too badly, even for a man who fixes everything.

Instead, it's Amelie, with a delicate Black woman about two inches shorter than her and a decade younger, dressed in deep colors and artsy silver jewelry.

Amelie's also brought my suitcase.

"Where's Seth?" I blurt before I can stop myself.

"Why would I know that?" Amelie's friend says nervously. "I don't know him. Never met him. Nope. No idea where he is or how he's paying for it—"

Amelie interrupts. "Belle, this is Barbie Emerson. She's with the FBI."

Belle waves at Barbie, her silver rings glinting.

"And this is Seth's Darcy." Amelie gestures to me.

I grimace. Seth's made it pretty obvious I'm *not* his, in any sense of the word.

"Darcy, this is my partner, Belle. I was hoping to introduce you all before…well."

Even Amelie can't find a way to summarize the last twenty-four hours tactfully. She coughs and passes me my suitcase as she turns to Barbie. "Barbie dear, will you point us to the restroom? I brought some things so Darcy can freshen up."

"That's not really regulation—"

"What am I going to do? Help her climb out a window? Smuggle her a weapon?" Amelie says.

Barbie puts her hands on her hips. "Just because—"

"Miss Emerson, I welcomed you into my home, knowing you were lying to me because I trusted my instinct about you. Now I'm asking you to repay the courtesy, trust your instincts, and let Darcy put on a damn bra before a transcontinental flight." Amelie raises her chin.

Barbie huffs. "Fine. Three minutes."

"Five. Eyeliner takes at least one minute," Amelie says as she shepherds me into the bathroom.

She's so determined about it, I half expect her to whip out an escape plan as soon as the door swings closed behind us. But no, she really does want to get me cleaned up. She passes me some face wipes from her purse that I use on my face, and then the rest of my body.

Getting clean should be the least of my priorities right now, but it feels like Amelie's turning me human again, with every bit of grime I wipe off.

Amelie attacks me with dry shampoo and starts fluffing my hair.

It's so ridiculous, it almost drags a smile out of me. "It's ok. I'm going to stuff it under a hat and throw on some sweats for the plane—"

"What? No," Amelie says, aghast.

She looks more upset than when she found out I was a criminal.

"No, you're wearing this," she says and rummages in my suitcase until she pulls out a red dress. It's a bright, bold, sleeveless A-line that falls to my knees and has the perfect twirl. I look at her face to see if she's joking, but she's dead serious.

"Amelie," I say. "I'm going to be sitting on a plane. For ten hours. Then I'm probably going to jail."

"That's why you're wearing flats instead of heels," Amelie says reasonably.

"Oh for Christ's sake." I reach for my pants, but Amelie blocks me, holding up the dry shampoo like it's pepper spray.

"You never know what the day will bring," she says stubbornly.

"Which is why you should always wear leggings," I say.

"*Dieu, sauve-moi des Américains,*" Amelie mutters. She hangs the dress on the stall and looks me up and down. "Come now. Where's the woman with the red boots and red lips that made my business-obsessed nephew spill his coffee?"

"Unemployed, dumped, and looking at life behind bars," I answer.

"Darcy. Have faith."

Something about the way she says it cracks through the last of my bravado. "I don't think I can. I tried to have hope, I did, and look where it got me." I spread my arms, helpless. "I don't think hope is for people like me. I should have run when I still could."

"No," she says, taking my face in her hands. "No, choosing to be brave is never wrong. And look what you won. Even if the worst should happen, you have your name back. And that is something Vivian LaBlanc never had."

My throat is tight as Amelie briskly steps back and digs into my suitcase until she finds my makeup bag.

"Now," Amelie says, "I am going to teach you what my mother taught me. You should always look ravishing. Ordinary days, celebrations. But especially when they're trying to tear you down."

She passes me the makeup bag before retrieving a gorgeous cream knee-length trench coat from my suitcase.

I blink. "That's not mine."

"I'm giving it to you. You need something to keep you warm on the plane. And it pairs beautifully with the red dress." Amelie holds out the coat for me.

All at once, I start sobbing. I swipe at my tears, trying to get control of myself. "Why are you being so kind to me?"

Amelie's smile is bittersweet. "I like you. I remember what it's like to be young and drowning. And I remember the women who showed me kindness. Although I must say, I didn't cry nearly as much as you."

I laugh through the tears.

Barbie bangs on the door. "Hurry up."

"Best do what she says before she confiscates the eyeliner," Amelie says.

I nod and splash water on my face until my breathing is under control. When I turn around, Amelie's holding up the red dress.

I take it. I put on the coat and the matching pointed-toe cream flats. I hang wispy gold from my ears and drape a barely-there chain around my neck. Amelie passes me my perfume like a captain arming her troops.

I keep my makeup subtle, but in deference to Amelie, I add a slash of red across my lips.

I meet her eyes in the mirror, and she gives a small, approving nod.

I roll back my shoulders, adjust the impossibly elegant coat she gave me, and accept my re-packed suitcase from her.

Amelie looks at my hand as I take the suitcase. Then she does something I wouldn't have expected from the sympathetic woman who just police-station-fairy-godmothered me.

Amelie smirks.

"What?" I ask.

"You say you have no hope. But you're still wearing that ring."

***

I don't say anything as Barbie drives us to Paris, the world slowly filling with gray and concrete as we get closer to the city. Barbie barks into her cell phone about some man who's gone off the grid. I stare out of the window and wish I were somewhere else.

I go through the airport numb, although I can't help smirking when Barbie gets pulled over as we go through security, for bringing her gun.

She's over in the corner arguing with airport security about permits when a lanky, red-haired man with kind eyes and a trusting smile jogs up to me.

"Psst! Miss, you dropped this," he says in a thick Scottish accent and holds out a battered, long black leather wallet to me.

I stare at it, then up at him.

"Uh… Pardon, mademoiselle," he mutters. "*Tu dinera mulleta.* Shit, that's Spanish. Bad Spanish. Please take it. It's got your ticket."

I flip the wallet open, and my heart slows. There's a French passport tucked into the wallet and a plane ticket to Australia. The ticket and passport are for Robin Jones, but it's my own photo staring up at me. There's a yellow sticky note tucked between the pages that reads "Truce. —V."

I'm already past security. If I ditch Barbie …

She's still arguing with the security guard.

Why would Victor help me disappear?

To keep me from testifying and further cooperating with the police.

The man checks his watch nervously. "We need to get back to the gate. They're boarding now."

My future is racing in front of me, like one of those roller-coaster sequences at a movie theater. On the one hand, jail, the US, everyone seeing me for who I am and knowing what I've done. On the other side, Australia. Freedom. A fresh start.

It's more than a line in the sand. It's a whole fucking ocean.

People like us fix our mistakes. We stay.

I want to tell the Seth in my head to shut up. He doesn't know me. He never did. *He* left *me.*

If I run, I'll never see him again.

If I stay, I still might never see him again. And I'll definitely see the inside of a jail cell.

I ball my hand into a fist, press it into my stomach. The din of the airport is roaring around me. Any second now, Barbie will look over here. I need to make a decision.

Then it's Amelie in my head, not Seth.

Have faith. Choosing to be brave is never wrong. You have your name back.

I am sick of signing someone else's name to my work, to my life. I am strong. I am tough.

I want my fucking name back.

I shake my head and hand the wallet back. "This isn't me," I say.

He flushes. "Christ. Fuck. I'm sorry. You look like the picture he sent. I swear I'm not one of those blokes who think all French girls look alike—"

"I'm American."

He turns around in fumbling humiliation, bashing into Barbie, and drops the wallet.

"Shit. Bugger. I'm sorry. I was trying to give the wallet back—"

Barbie grabs the wallet. She flips it open, looks at me.

Her eyes narrow. "Why, you little—"

"It's not mine," I protest.

But she's already whipping out the cuffs. She claps one on my wrist, one on hers, muttering about stupid countries with their stupid weapons restrictions and how I'm getting on her last good nerve.

I look to my gangly Scottish friend for support, but he's already disappeared.

***

There's no reasoning with Barbie. Getting down the airplane aisle and getting our suitcases up in the luggage rack is slapstick comedy gold.

A pompous-looking middle-aged man a few rows over looks down his nose at me as we settle into our seats, so I wink at him and mouth "role play," before Barbie shoves me down into the window seat, takes the middle seat, and bullies the person on the aisle into requesting a different seat.

I slump back, my amusement waning as the plane slowly prepares for takeoff.

It's going to be a long flight. And on the other side…

On the other side is my name, I tell myself firmly.

The roar of the plane taking off swells around me, the pressure pushing me back into my seat. The friction of wheels on pavement builds, and then suddenly everything releases as we're lifted into the sky.

I feel a strange exhilaration as the lights of the city dance and slide beneath us. I feel like laughing. Or breaking something. Celebrating. Weeping.

For better or worse, I'm not the same person I was. I'll never be her again.

When the flight attendant comes around, asking if we want anything, I'm already shoving my credit card at her.

"Champagne. Lots of it. Also ice cream. Do you have ice cream? How about chocolate? Cheese?" I think about sitting across from Seth in the cafe, eating the most decadent chocolate in the world while he looked at me like *that*.

There's a flinch of pain in my general heart region.

"Maybe not chocolate," I say.

"*Non. Elle est une criminelle—*" Barbie starts.

"Yes, I'm a criminal," I interrupt, exasperated. "My name is Darcy Sherwood. I've been dumped by the best man I've ever loved. I've had one fake marriage and one fake engagement. I'm the best art forger in a generation. I'm probably going to jail when this plane lands. So if you have any mercy at all, give me all the champagne, cheese, ice cream, and potato chips you have."

The woman blinks, then takes my credit card. She hands me four personal bottles of champagne and a plastic cup. "I'll be back with your food."

Because I'm a good person, I fill the cup and pass it to Barbie. I finish off the bottle in one swig and start on the next one.

"Is it horrible to admit I like you?" Barbie asks wryly.

"Probably Stockholm syndrome. Or Lima syndrome. I forget which is which." I wrestle with the cork on the next bottle.

I grab my purse because I never actually finished that romance novel. But when I look, it's not there.

"I can't drink this," Barbie says. "I'm on duty."

"We both recently survived the weirdest vacation of our entire lives. Live a little." *And I need someone to talk to, so I don't think of waking up on Seth's shoulder, under his jacket.*

"Oh, what the hell. One glass," Barbie says as she takes a sip. "But you have to share the potato chips."

"Deal," I say, and I clink my bottle with her plastic cup.

Chapter Twenty-One

Seth

My leg's going up and down like a jackhammer as I ride the N train out to Astoria. I have to get to that apartment. If I'm right...if Victor's got evidence there that could get the charges against Darcy dropped...

I watch the skyline fly by as the train goes aboveground. I clutch my briefcase. As we leave Manhattan the buildings get shorter, squarer, more brick, more graffiti.

It's surreal, taking this part of the line again. I used to take it every day when I first moved to the States. This part used to mean I was almost home.

Now it means I'm almost to enemy territory, where my brother's the enemy.

The train comes to a stop, and I rush out onto the platform, through the gate, across the overpass. The wind from the cars racing below chills my bones.

There are more Instagrammable restaurants than there used to be, and my old favorite diner has a "sold" sign in the window. I cut across the small square park and head over to my old building.

It's got a keycard entrance, so I call every apartment on the callbox and tell them I have their delivery order until someone lets me in.

The stairwell is cold and draughty, the tile stained and broken in places, freshly repaired in others. It's a six-floor walk-up, and my old place is at the top.

I race up to the top, taking the stairs two at a time. My heart pounds as I feel for the crack of broken wood on the top of the door frame where Victor always hid a spare key after he got locked out once and couldn't get a hold of the apartment manager for a whole weekend.

For a second I think it's not there, and my heart plummets, but then my fingers find the cold, irregular edge of metal.

I grab the key and, after checking no one's watching, unlock the door and push it open. I step inside.

It's an old, narrow studio. It used to be filled with cheap, broken furniture because I'd spent all my money on unframed paintings I'd stacked carefully against the walls. It used to be warm, and mine.

Now it's eerily empty, except for one painting hanging against the wall at the end of the long, narrow room. I stare at it, trying to figure out what's wrong until I remember. There used to be a built-in cabinet shelf there.

I cross to the painting and take it down. The shelf is gone. In its place is a safe.

My pulse picks up. I was right. Victor keeps something important here.

Now all I need to do is figure out the combination.

I try his birthday, his graduation year, the date his first gallery opened. I even try the day he lost his virginity because unfortunately, I know that. I try every number combination of significance to him, but for once in my brother's selfish life, it's not about him.

Of course not. That would be bad security.

Hmm. A date important to someone Victor likes...

I try my mom's birthday. There's a tiny click on the first number, and my heart speeds up, but the rest of the date doesn't work. I try it again, but it doesn't work.

I slam my hand into the wall, defeated. The whole plan rests on getting this evidence.

Stop being a drama king, Darcy says in my head. *Use that uptight brain of yours.*

Right. I take a deep breath. I have the first number. Now I need to figure the rest out.

What number starts with an eight, and matters to Victor?

I snort. There's my birthday, obviously, but he wouldn't— I reach for the dial and try my birthday. 8th December 1987.

The safe clicks open, and I blink, shocked. He hasn't so much as wished me a happy birthday since he tried to frame me.

Maybe this is another attempt at framing me. The apartment I lived in. A safe with my birth date.

I open the safe, hands trembling. Inside, there's a worn leather journal. I reach for it before I remember at the last second to put gloves on, so I don't contaminate the evidence.

I flip through the journal gently. The leather gloves make my fingers clumsy with the pages, but I can see enough. The whole thing is filled with what looks like a ledger, except it's written in absolute gibberish.

Unless… I look closer.

It's a code we came up with as children, one summer at Amelie's. Not particularly sophisticated, but enough to keep people guessing for a day or so until Victor could get the ledger back or destroy it if it fell into the hands of someone who didn't know the code.

The only other person who knows the code is…me.

I slam the book closed and look up to see the red light of a camera at the back of the safe.

Shit. If it's a live feed he'll know…

I need to get out of here.

I stuff the ledger in my briefcase and rip off my gloves as I race out of the apartment, only to have a man grab my throat and throw me back into the landing wall.

It's Victor, looking angrier than I've ever seen him in my life.

He didn't need a video feed to warn him. He knows me too well.

I rub my throat. He's blocking the stairs. For the first time in my life, I am physically frightened of my brother.

Lie, Seth, Darcy says in my head. *Lie.*

I slouch, defeated. "You don't have to look at me like that," I say, letting all the bitter, poisoned fury I've felt for years seep into my voice. "I couldn't get the safe open. Darcy's going to prison. Because of you—"

He yanks the apartment door open, to check if what I'm saying is true. It's only a second, but it's all I need to race past him down the stairs. He makes a grab for my collar and misses, losing his balance and tumbling down the stairs, slamming into me. I grab for the railing, and it breaks under my weight, the iron ripping from the brick.

I'm falling back through the air—six stories to a cement floor—when Victor grabs my hand. For a moment I'm ten, falling down the stairs, and my big brother's got me.

And then I slip in his grasp. I weigh more than I did then, and he's got a hell of a better reason to drop me.

"Drop the briefcase," Victor pants, his face going red from the effort of keeping me from falling.

"What?"

"Drop the briefcase, and grab that bit of railing, there, that's newer."

"But what if it breaks—"

"I've got your other hand."

I hesitate.

His feet slip a hairsbreadth on the tile stairs. "Come on, you fucker."

Somehow Victor swearing at me is enough to make me trust him.

I drop the briefcase and grab the base of the guardrail that hasn't broken.

"One," I say.

"Two," he says.

"Three," we say together, and he pulls as I use the railing to hoist my core onto the stairs. Victor grabs my torso and yanks me the rest of the way onto the stairs.

It's not dignified, but we get safely onto solid ground. Victor collapses next to me, breathing hard. "Jesus. Don't *do* that to me. She's only a girl, and probably long gone by now. She's not worth dying over."

I look at him. My brother, who was everything I wanted to be. Until, abruptly, he wasn't. "Then turn yourself in. Stop making me do stupid shit to catch you."

He laughs, but it's broken. "You're never going to be mean enough to catch me, Seth." He gives me a giant hug, fierce, like it might be the last one he ever gives me.

I can't help it. I hug him back. I don't *want* to do what I'm about to do.

I give him one final squeeze because God knows he's not going to want to hug me after today, and there's a click behind my head.

He's handcuffed me to the railing. With fuzzy pink handcuffs. I look at him in horror.

Victor smirks. "Barbie wasn't always a born-again virgin."

"Ewwwww."

Victor stands, and jogs down the stairs toward the briefcase, hugging the wall and staying well away from the railing.

"Victor, wait," I yell. "Turn yourself in and I'll get you the best lawyers. I'll get you a deal. Please, they're going to catch you."

A few people are cautiously popping their heads out of their apartments now.

"Fuck, Victor, listen to me," I bellow. "Don't take the briefcase."

His steps fade away, and there's the heavy slam of the door downstairs. When I take a deep breath and make myself peek over the ledge, Victor and the briefcase are gone.

A freakishly muscled man approaches me, and I wince, but he bends down and snaps the fuzzy pink handcuffs in two.

"I've tried these before," he says. "Not very strong. Go check out Babeland. They can get you better stuff."

I babble a thank you and race down the stairs, my heart in my throat. Either this worked, or I've lost Darcy's last shot at freedom.

I open the door and see Victor, briefcase in hand, surrounded by every arts reporter in the city who owes me a favor.

"What's in the briefcase, Mr. Moreau?"

"There have been accusations you were the leader in an impressionist forgery ring five years ago. Do you have a comment?"

"Your brother Seth Moreau accused you of the highest-profile art crime of the decade. Why would he do that?"

"I can answer that," I say, walking toward the gaggle of reporters. "It's because someone innocent is taking the fall for my brother's crimes. While I love him, I'm done letting him hurt people I care about."

I take my briefcase back from Victor's unprotesting fingers and pull out the ledger.

I hold it up for at least three TV stations to document, spreading it open so they can get a shot of a tiny slice of Victor's crimes.

"You're still in love with her," Victor hisses accusingly. "Even after you found out who she really is."

"I love you, even after finding out who you really are," I say reasonably, and I hear a reporter laugh. Apparently we're not being as quiet as we thought.

"What are you going to do? Profess your undying love during prison visiting hours?" Victor asks snidely as the sound of sirens approaches.

"No. I've got a better idea."

And then I turn back to the cameras, prepared to tell the people of New York the biggest lie of my life.

Darcy would be so proud.

Chapter Twenty-Two

Darcy

Barbie and I have made it through customs—both a little hung over from the flight—when I notice men giving me a second glance. At first, I think it's Amelie's makeover, but then I see some kids looking at me and pointing.

Can they see the handcuffs? I've been trying to hide them in the sleeves of my coat, but the chain is still hanging in front of my skirt.

Barbie's phone rings. "Yes, ma'am, I've got her. We've landed... No, I haven't turned on a TV..." She cranes her neck, looking for one of the TVs posted all over the airport. When she finds one, she gasps.

I follow her gaze. For a second I wonder if maybe I'm still drunk.

Seth's on TV, holding up some sort of notebook filled with Victor's handwriting, although what he's written doesn't even look like a language. In the background, Victor's being arrested and shoved into a car. An FBI agent appears and takes the notebook from Seth.

The screen cuts back to a news anchor.

"The FBI arrested alleged art forgery ringleader Victor Moreau earlier today when his older brother turned him in. When asked why he would do this, Seth Moreau said he figured it out when the FBI arrested the wrong woman—Seth Moreau's former secretary, Darcy Smith."

My company ID photo flashes across the screen. I'm two years younger in a soft white blouse, my eyes hesitant but hopeful. Eager to please.

I look like a total mark. Why the hell would Seth give them that photo?

The screen cuts back to Seth, looking square-jawed and handsome in his glasses. Very Gregory Peck.

"My brother first preyed on Darcy when she was an art student, still a minor."

I blink. That's not true.

"She thought he was legitimately interested in her art. As soon as she found out the truth, she tried to get out, and got a job working with me. She didn't tell anyone what she'd survived. When my brother found out where Darcy was working, he followed us to Europe, where he convinced a young, inexperienced FBI agent Darcy was the one who had been running the ring."

Seth shakes his head sadly, then looks straight at the camera. "The FBI might prefer to blame a young woman single-handedly masterminded an art forgery ring—when she couldn't even afford to graduate college—rather than a rich, powerful man who's been donating to law enforcement agencies for years. But I'm done letting corruption like that flourish in my city, no matter who it is. I think most New Yorkers agree with me."

There's another photo of me, looking around Monet's garden in wonder. It's juxtaposed with a blurry photo of Victor lounging at a nightclub, martini in hand, eyes hallowed, dripping reckless wealth, judging the world.

The news anchor shakes her head in faux concern. "Reports say Miss Smith is *still* being held in custody. And now, onto our top story tonight: Can expired sunscreen kill you?"

I stare up at the TV, stunned. Seth lied for me. To all of New York City. *On live TV.*

Of course, he'll have to issue a correction tomorrow, because those lies are pretty damn checkable, but few people will care about some dry statement. He's making it politically costly for the FBI to hold me.

He's spent years building up credit as responsible, restrained. Now he's cashing in that reputation to save me.

His words come back to me, words I was scared to believe. *I love you, Darcy. I am desperately head over heels for you.*

I haven't lost him. If my hands weren't cuffed, I'd wrap my arms around myself, hug the knowledge to me.

Although speaking of the cuffs... People are definitely staring. But more and more of them are looking at me with sympathy, and glaring at Barbie, who's turned away from everybody, hissing into her phone.

"The story he's feeding the press is crap. I didn't arrest her for running the ring, I arrested her for forgery, which she confessed to... Yes.... Yes ma'am... What do you mean he won't translate it unless she's released? Are we seriously giving in to him?"

The volume on the other end of the phone increases dramatically, and Barbie winces.

Someone takes a photo of me and Barbie.

"You know," I point out quietly, "if even one photo of me and you goes viral, you can never work undercover again."

Barbie's eyes widen in horror, and she marches me around the corner and into a bathroom stall, muttering, "Yes ma'am," into her phone at random intervals the whole time.

She unlocks the cuffs as the yelling on the other end of the phone winds to a close.

"Yes ma'am. I understand. She's been released. I have her statements and contact information if we want to charge her later... Yes ma'am. Yes, I understand. No charges."

She hangs up and looks at me. "I can't tell if you and Seth are honest idiots in love, or if I'm being played by master manipulators."

I bite the inside of my cheek to keep from smiling. "No comment."

***

I'm heading down the sidewalk, stride sure, head held high, cream coat flapping in the wind. Freer than I've ever been.

The FBI knows what I've done, and they're not charging me. Seth knows what I've done, and he still went to bat for me. Amelie knows, and she still cared enough to wash my face.

The city is singing around me. Cab horns, bike bells, radios playing. Spring means people are rolling down their windows, letting the world hear their song.

And me?

I'm high on hope, on freedom, on having a future. I could literally sing from the joy of it all. Or paint a mural. Something big. Something uncontainable.

This may be the only feeling in the world better than being in love.

I spin around in a circle, delighted, and a man bashes into me, dropping his briefcase, the contents spilling out.

"Oops, sorry, I—" I trail off as I see the book peeking out of the briefcase.

It's my romance novel. When I look up, I realize it's Seth crouched next to me, grabbing papers.

He looks at me head to toe, and swallows.

"Darcy. I'm sorry. I was going to meet you at the airport, but it took forever to get the FBI to agree—"

"You lied to everyone for me," I cut him off.

"You told the truth for me," he says simply. His eyes are bright behind his glasses, drinking me in, and my stomach flips.

I stand, and he follows.

"Look," he says abruptly. "I'm sorry I didn't listen. I'm so fucking sorry I left you alone at the station—"

"Yeah," I say. "That hurt."

His hand lifts reflexively like he wants to reach out, but he holds himself back.

"I'm sorry I didn't trust you," I say. "You asked if he was blackmailing me, and promised to help, and I didn't tell you. I was so scared..." I swallow. "I was scared you wouldn't love me if you knew."

"Oh Darcy," he says. He steps toward me and gently tucks a curl behind my ear. I close my eyes and breathe with relief because he's touching me again.

"I'm afraid I'm at the unconditional stage of love," Seth says matter-of-factly. "It's not because you're beautiful, or because you're a brilliant and honest professional, or a brilliant and crooked forger. It's not because you're brave, or funny, or because you were willing to go to jail to protect me."

He takes my face in his hands, and his breath is a little unsteady when he says, "It's you, Darcy Sherwood. Dump as much coffee on me as you want. I love you. Thoroughly, miserably, unconditionally."

I grab him and kiss him. I kiss the bravest, kindest, best man I know. He tastes like home and adventure, all at once. I sink my hands into his hair, trying to touch as much of him as I can.

Seth wraps his arms around me like he never wants to let me go. His stubble scrapes against the soft skin under my lip.

"I love you, so much, Seth," I say. "And for me, it's you, like you said, not because of—"

"I know," he says.

"How?" I demand.

Seth grins. It's a brilliant, carefree grin. He looks as light and happy as I feel as he takes my hand, kisses it, then grabs my suitcase in one fluid moment.

"You're not a subtle woman when you love someone, Darcy. I was scared to believe it." He kisses my hand again, then hesitates. I realize I'm still wearing his ring.

"Sorry about that," I say. "I meant to move it to my right hand."

"Leave it," he says, and I nearly drop the book I'm holding.

My heart is pounding so fast I think it's going to sprout wings and turn into a hummingbird. He looks calm and casual, but I know he means it, because his hand has tightened around mine in a death grip.

"Uh-uh," I say, because I'm not ready to say yes today, but I'm sure as hell not saying no. "You're not getting off that easy. I earned this ring fair and square. You want a real wife, I want a real proposal."

"Ah yes," Seth says, as we start walking. "I believe I'm supposed to be overcome by emotion after making passionate love to you?"

"*That* was merely a suggestion."

"I think my use of the media today shows I'm quite comfortable stealing your ideas," Seth says, and I throw my head back and laugh.

"Where are we going?"

"To my place. We're going to eat, and sleep, and shower, and practice the first step of that proposal. Not necessarily in that order." He grins down at me. "Unless you have any objections?"

I lean my head happily on his arm as we wait for the crosswalk light to turn.

"No objections," I say. "But a question. And I want you to tell me the truth."

Seth hears the seriousness in my voice and turns to face me. "Anything," he says. He lifts my chin, and kisses me softly, surely, before pulling away to look me squarely in the eyes. "Anything at all."

"Why do you have my romance novel?"

Epilogue

Seth

There's always something about Amelie's chateau that makes me feel peaceful, right.

And being back here with Darcy, who looks like a dream in a frothy, pastel pink vintage gown, as she waits by an arched flower trellis for the wedding photography to wrap up so the party can start?

It's pretty damn perfect.

When Amelie couldn't get her deposits for our fake double wedding back, she persuaded the vendors to reschedule (possibly using tactics she learned from Darcy) for the end of summer, and marry Belle, since she'd basically been designing her own dream wedding anyway.

It's been fun to meet all of Belle and Amelie's friends and to introduce Darcy to my parents. I don't know if my mum will ever forgive me for turning in Victor, who's in prison in upstate New York serving out a ten-year sentence, although I heard a rumor he might be able to shorten his sentence by working with Barbie as an informant on forgery cases. But after seeing me with Darcy, Mum's beginning to soften.

Barbie's here, looking fabulous in a black sundress with pockets and sky-high cheetah-print high heels. Apparently her affinity for cheetah print was not part of her undercover work.

Darcy's and my eyes meet, and I go to her without thinking. We may have broadened our respective social circles in the last few months (now she's no longer hiding a secret identity, and I'm no longer stewing over Victor's betrayal), but Darcy's still my favorite person in the world.

I'm so damn proud of her. She took some of the money I gave her to start a fund for low-income art school students.

She's also officially divorced from Mr. Smith, thank God.

Darcy's using the rest of the money to live on while she gives herself time to paint. After the attention she got from Victor's arrest, there's been more interest in her work, but Darcy's holding off on selling anything for now, until she finds "her voice."

But every painting she makes, even the bad ones, she signs with triumphant relish.

It's one of the many reasons I'll be asking her to marry me tonight, after the ceremony, when all the guests have left. I got Amelie's blessing to cover the maze in candles and rose petals. Then, when we get to the center, I'll ask her to marry me.

I hope she says yes. I'm giddy with hope shot through with nerves. Did I mention Darcy tells me she loves me every day? Because she does. Darcy Sherwood loves *me*. The evidence is everywhere, in the brilliantly colored shoes piling up by my door, and the way she keeps my staid shirts in a place of honor in her closet once reserved for a certain backless evening gown.

I lean in to kiss Darcy, and she laughs and shoves me away. "Mr. Moreau. You'll smear my makeup."

"Is that a dare?" I ask.

Something in her face changes and I wonder if being back here has her thinking too. Of all the ways we've changed since I first brought her to the chateau, and all the ways we haven't.

"No," Darcy says. She wraps my tie around her fist and rises up until her soft, wicked, miracle lips are a hair's breadth from mine. "It's a demand. Meet me in the heart of the maze in two minutes."

***

The sound of the party falls away as I move deeper into the maze. It's only the soft fall of my feet on the grass now.

I hesitate before the final turn. Darcy's on the other side of the hedge, waiting for me.

I take a deep breath.

Now or never.

When I round the bend, I see Darcy walking barefoot over rose petals, her heels dangling from her fingertips. For a moment I can't

188

breathe. She's that kind of wonderful, and I'm kind of terrified she'll say no.

Darcy sees me, and her face lights up. Suddenly I can breathe again because she's smiling at me.

"Seth, someone's covered everything with rose petals..." She trails off as I drop down to one knee.

"Don't suppose you're looking for a husband?" I ask, trying for charming even though my mouth has gone dry.

Darcy raises a hand to her mouth, her eyes softening as she looks at me.

Any impulse toward cockiness vanishes. When she's wearing her heart on her face like that, I can't be anything else but deeply, plainly honest. "Because I'd love to marry you, Darcy. I can't think of anything in the world I want more. But if that's not what you're looking for, this seems as good a time as any to tell you I will love you, Darcy Sherwood, until my dying day."

She takes my face and kisses me breathless, her tears and laughter falling on my face like a sun shower.

"Only if it's you," Darcy says, and my heart leaps. "Because I intend to love you, Seth Moreau, until long after my dying day."

"Only you would turn a proposal into a competition." I stand and slide the ring onto her finger. It's not as fine as the last one—I'm roughly a half-million poorer than I was the last time I went ring shopping—but Darcy holds up her hand like it's the most precious thing in the world.

"Should we take a picture?" she asks. "I'm so happy, I feel like I need to shove it into other people's lives, or I'm going to explode."

I laugh and reach for my phone.

***

It takes way longer to take this photo than our fake engagement one did, because I can't stop kissing Darcy. Finally, Darcy gives up and snaps a photo while I'm kissing her.

In the photo, I'm standing behind Darcy, my arms wrapped around her as I kiss the corner of her smile, and Darcy looks up at the camera, smug like we're going to be happy forever.

It's the most real thing in the world.

ABOUT THE AUTHOR

Kate is passionate about using storytelling to bring more joy and hope into people's lives. She's ghostwritten several independently published contemporary romance novels for various clients. *The Last Big Fake* is her first novel under her own name. She's worked in the arts as a marketing associate at Portland Center Stage at The Armory and Oregon Ballet Theatre. She holds a B.A. from American University in political science, with a minor in communications, and volunteers for Women for the Win.

Connect with Kate:
website: katekernswrites.com
IG @katekernswrites
FB: facebook.com/katekernswrites
twitter: @katekernswrites

www.BOROUGHSPUBLISHINGGROUP.com

If you enjoyed this book, please write a review. Our authors appreciate the feedback, and it helps future readers find books they love. We welcome your comments and invite you to send them to info@boroughspublishinggroup.com. Follow us on Facebook, Twitter and Instagram, and be sure to sign up for our newsletter for surprises and new releases from your favorite authors.

Are you an aspiring writer? Check out www.boroughspublishinggroup.com/submit and see if we can help you make your dreams come true.

www.ingramcontent.com/pod-product-compliance
Lightning Source LLC
Chambersburg PA
CBHW061206170626
46809CB00003B/1262